Tale Half Told

The Encounter Series

The Encounter Series:

1971: Tale Half Told

1985: The Encounter (coming soon)

Also by Killarney Traynor:

Summer Shadows

Necessary Evil

Michael Lawrence: the Season of Darkness

Tale Half Told

The Encounter Series

Story by:

Margaret Traynor and Killarney Traynor

Written by :

Killarney Traynor

This is a work of fiction.

Names, characters, businesses, organizations, places, events, and incidents are either products of the author's imagination, or are used fictiously. Any resemblance to actual events, locales, organizations, or persons (living or dead) is entirely coincidental.

Christmas Cover Design by James, GoOnWrite.com

Haunted House Cover designed by Killarney Traynor

There in seclusion and remote from men
The wizard hand lies cold,
Which at its topmost speed let fall the pen
And left the tale half told.
            - *Longfellow*

"How it is that I appear before you in a shape that you can see, I may not tell. I have sat invisible beside you many and many a day."
            - *Dickens, 'A Christmas Carol'*

CONTENTS

CAST OF CHARACTERS:

1946:

Charles Reynolds, *the war veteran, deceased*

Helene Reynolds, *his war-bride, deceased*

Lionel Reynolds, *Charles' grandfather, deceased*

Rachel Reynolds, *Charles' great-aunt,*

Jacob North, *the orphan, Lionel's ward*

Irene Simmons North, *Jacob's wife, deceased*

1971:

Michael Wright, *a distant cousin of the Reynolds*

Susan Wright, *his wife, a nurse*

Linda Vincent, *Susan's school friend, also a nurse*

Johnny Vincent, *Linda's brother, a Vietnam War vet*

William Emery, *a local cop*

PROLOGUE

Article in the **Triple Town Sentry**, *December 15th, 1971:*

Reynolds Mansion Slated for Demolition

The 25th anniversary of the murder-suicide of Charles and Helene Reynolds may be celebrated by the leveling of the historic Reynolds mansion.

Reynolds Development Corporation has expressed interest in developing the Reynolds estate on Winnabenaki River into a resort. While this would be a boon for a region with little industry or tourism, some of the locals hope the old mansion, known as River House, will be spared.

"River House is a part of our history," said Gloria Stark, owner of a small farm on the outskirts of town. "I remember the fine parties they used to have there when I was a child. I know we need the tourism, but I don't know why anyone would want to destroy the house. It's part of the landscape now. If it weren't for that incident, they would still be using it."

This December 23rd marks the 25th anniversary of the murder-suicide that rocked the state. Charles Reynolds, son and heir to the Reynolds land development empire, was a war hero freshly returned from Germany. Reynolds killed his wife, Helene Reynolds, during the family's annual Christmas party, and then threw himself into Winnabenaki River. The current president of the company, Jacob North, was also present that night and nearly drowned in an attempt to save Charles. Guests at the party were united in grief. The tragedy earned the nick-name, the Othello killing, as it was thought Charles had killed his wife out of jealousy regarding her supposed affair. The affair was never proven, making the murder seem all the more tragic. Local legend claims that River House is now haunted by the ghost of Charles Reynolds, who wanders the halls in eternal regret of his rash actions.

On being questioned about the ghostly legend, Mrs. Stark laughed. "Sane people don't believe in ghosts anymore, do they?"

The Othello murder-suicide is not the only tragedy connected to River House. Jacob North's wife, Irene Simmons North, fell to her death ten years ago when she lost her footing on a staircase. The house has since been deserted and now sits as a lonely, haunted reminder of past opulence and tragedy.

Development of the property hinges on the decision of Rachel Reynolds, the current owner of River House and its last occupant. It is rumored the current project proposal has been rejected by Ms. Reynolds, however details are difficult to confirm. She is currently in Tampa, Florida, and was unavailable for questioning at the time of publication.

Part One:
ISOLATION

CHAPTER 1

It was Michael's idea to make the detour. It was mid-afternoon on December 23rd, a bright and sunny day that was starting to turn gray with the promise of snow. He and his wife, Susan, were driving with their two friends to her parent's summer house on Winnipesauke to spend the Christmas holiday. They had only a half hour left to their trip when he suggested it.

The idea did not have much appeal to his passengers. They had all been in the car for several hours since leaving Massachusetts and had only stopped once to gas up and get lunch at a small diner in New Hampshire. The farther north they went, the colder it got, until even the sedan's fine heating system struggled to keep the levels comfortable.

Michael Wright, a tall, lanky man with energy that belied his rather mundane profession of accountant, was desperate to get out of the car and stretch his legs. 1971 had been a very good year for him. He had married, moved into a house in a nice neighborhood, and, having worked for the prestigious Reynolds Development Company for two years, qualified for a promotion and a fat Christmas bonus. The Wright star, he was convinced, was on the rise and he was as eager as a child to explore some place new.

"It'll be a quick stop," he promised his passengers who were wedged tightly between bags, wrapped presents, and Tupperware filled with snacks for the upcoming holiday. "It's only twenty minutes out of our way."

Susan, Michael's girlfriend since Boston University and wife since June, objected. "It's going to storm tonight. I don't want to be caught out in the road in a nor'easter. Let's stop on the way back."

"We aren't coming back this way," he said. "We're taking the coastal route home, remember? And take a look at that sky. It's not going to snow for hours. What do you say, Linda, Johnny?" He addressed the semi-comatose couple in the back. "Want to see a haunted house?"

"Oh, *Michael*!" Susan punched him lightly on the shoulder.

Linda Vincent, reclining in the back seat with a magazine and a cigarette, leaned forward with sudden interest. Her reddish-brown hair, stick straight as modern style would have it, gleamed in the afternoon light, highlighted by the navy blue wool jacket she wore. Leather boots, a denim skirt, and a gold-colored turtleneck sweater completed her outfit.

"Haunted?" she asked, her tired brown eyes suddenly alight with new energy. "Come on, don't be an idiot, Michael."

"What?" He grinned at her in the rear view mirror. "Nurses aren't supposed to believe in the paranormal?"

"We're trained in the sciences," Susan reminded him. "Science doesn't trust the unprovable." She twisted in her seat to face Linda. "Michael doesn't want to see it because he believes in ghosts. It's the old River House itself that he's interested in."

Linda's brother, Johnny, sat up now. He was a stocky man with a close-cropped haircut that betrayed his military profession. His eyes were a murkier shade than his sister's. Johnny was only a year out of Vietnam and Susan thought that if anyone ought to be kept away from a haunted location, it was him.

"I've read about this place, haven't I?" he asked, showing his first sign of interest in anything since the Wrights picked him up earlier that day. "Wasn't there something in the news about River House?"

"Yeah, a gossipy article in one of the papers," Michael replied, shifting briskly. "There was a lot of talk in the office about whether the Old Man had seen it yet."

The Old Man was Jacob North, president of Reynolds Development Company, where Michael worked.

"Tacky of them, mentioning his wife's accident like that," Susan said.

"Yeah, the guys in marketing weren't too happy about it."

"So what's the story about this place?" Linda asked. "I don't know a thing about it."

"It's the Reynolds family estate, held in trust by the last surviving member, Rachel Reynolds," Michael said, pleased to be able to tell the story again. "The Reynolds own practically that whole stretch of river, you know, and RDC is going to build the vacation destination of the North East; fishing and canoeing in the summer, easy access to skiing in the winter. The place is a gold mine."

"Michael's been talking about nothing else for months." Susan gave her husband an affectionate shove.

Even so, she worried about this turn in the conversation. It had been her idea to invite the Vincents for Christmas. Linda was her best friend, orphaned at a young age, and coping with a brother whose night terrors were so intense as to require occasional hospitalization. Susan thought that they could use an excuse to get out of the city and to some place without a personal history.

Now she wondered if this trip was a good idea. Johnny was reported to be doing better lately, but was spending a Christmas holiday in an isolated house really the best therapy for him? Looking into his eyes, Susan doubted it. She could see he was haunted by reality as well as nightmares.

Mom's house will be full of people, she reminded herself, adjusting her suede coat and pressing a hand against her slightly nauseous stomach. *At least Linda won't have to cope alone.*

"So you want to go and just pay this Rachel Reynolds a visit?" Johnny asked skeptically. He was dressed entirely in black, except for his jeans, and he rolled his gloves in his hands as he spoke.

"Rachel's in Florida," Michael replied. "The place is empty."

Of the four, he was the one best dressed for the holiday: tan coat over a bright holiday sweater and slacks. He drove with the ease of someone who had been raised in long, hard winters where four months of snow-covered roads were a given.

"Why do you want to see this place?" Linda asked. "What's in there, buried treasure?"

"Not very likely – North's as tight a man as you'll ever meet. If there was treasure he would have found it somehow. Being wheelchair-bound the past fifteen years hasn't slowed him down a bit."

"Then why?"

"I've been reading and studying about it for months. I'm curious, but they don't send accountants to check on the properties." He shifted again, slowing as the bends in the road became sharper. "I'll tell you one thing, though: the engineers who went up to survey the property didn't like River House. They called it spooky – wouldn't even go inside it."

"Given its reputation, I'm not surprised," Johnny said. "How long has Rachel been gone?"

"Ten years," Michael said. "It's been boarded up and left to rot ever since Mrs. North fell down that flight of steps. It'll be completely empty, I promise. No one will even know we've been there."

"Isn't that breaking and entering?" Susan asked fretfully.

"Not if we don't break anything," Michael said. "Oh, look, here's the turn."

And he took it.

CHAPTER 2

It was, as Michael had promised, only twenty minutes to the old house.

Linda yawned and shifted in her seat. She had just come off of an overnight shift at the hospital and catnapping in the cramped sedan was not enough to restore her energy. Judging from the drawn look on Johnny's face, he was tired too, although he would never have admitted it. Weakness was something that Johnny despised, especially in himself. Ever since childhood he had tried making himself into a stoic superman. In Linda's opinion, this mindset was Johnny's greatest obstacle to coming to terms with whatever had happened overseas.

For now, however, he looked as peaceful as he ever did. He spoke with Michael, leaning forward, his eyes glinting with interest.

Good, Linda thought. *He's coming out of himself.*

She leaned back and looked out the window. Snowdrifts piled high along the sides of the road. Bare, black elms and maples jutted up from the snow to claw at the sky, while evergreens provided welcome green relief. The sky was blue with heavy, gray clouds moving in from the mountains. Susan was right, as she usually was, about the storm coming. It was going to be a doozy when it got here.

Susan had twisted around in her seat to talk to Johnny. Her face was framed by thick blond ringlets, artfully left out from her bun, and her huge brown eyes were serious. She was four years younger than Linda and her best friend since college, Linda having started her schooling late. Of the two, Susan was the mother hen, with a loyal heart, a fiercely protective nature, and the looks of a TV star. At times Linda was intimidated by her. Susan was one of those girls who always knew what she was doing, where she was going, and how she was going to look when she got there. By contrast, Linda's life was a train wreck.

Once Linda had hoped they would be in-laws. Susan and Johnny were the same age and they would have been a handsomely matched set. But her brother, despite his sensitive side, had always been an army-man in the making. Anyway, once Michael appeared on the scene, Susan could see no one else.

Probably for the best, Linda thought now, looking at Johnny. *His condition would be an overwhelming challenge for newlyweds. not that Susan couldn't handle it. She can handle anything.*

It was not the first time Linda found herself relieved not to have the Perfect Woman for a sister-in-law. Despite this, Susan was a good friend and her marriage to Michael hadn't changed her relationship with Linda, which was something of a miracle. Everyone knew that marriages were the death knell for single-friendships.

When River House came into view, Linda could see at once why the locals thought it haunted. It was a large, rambling Victorian, shuttered and dark with a profile that would have given Vincent Price the creeps. Standing on top of a small rise, it towered over them as Michael carefully worked his way up the steep, unplowed drive. When the house's shadow touched the car, Linda felt a sudden drop in temperature. But it was only Michael, lowering his window for a better look.

"There she is," he said, in a hushed tone that would have been ominous had he not been grinning like a kid. He threw on the brakes, turned off the car, and waved towards the building. "The old Reynolds Manor, site of so much fear, terror, and tragedy."

"You shouldn't joke about it, Michael," Susan snapped. "It was a terrible thing."

The note in Susan's tone was abnormally harsh. She looked ashen when Linda glanced at her.

"What happened here, exactly?" Johnny asked. His voice was quiet and taut.

"Murder and suicide," Michael said and then he was out the door, wading through the shifting snow piles toward the front door.

"What is he doing?" Susan asked fretfully. She was stroking her stomach again, Linda noticed.

Johnny was getting out, too.

"Come on, Lin," he said, just before he slammed the car door shut. "Let's stretch our legs."

The two women sat in the car alone, watching the men make their way up the path to the front porch. Overhead, the wind moved the trees, making the cold wood creak. The house was a silent black silhouette on the grey and white landscape. When one could tear their eyes off of the house, Winnabenaki River spread out before them in serene, frozen glory, with New Hampshire's famed mountains in the background. It was a sight that should have inspired awe. It served, instead, to remind Linda of how isolated they were.

Linda leaned forward and touched Susan's shoulder, apologizing automatically when the woman jumped.

"What's going on here, Susie?" she asked.

Susan sighed deeply and her warm eyes looked sad. "Michael's been obsessed with this place for weeks," she said. "It's all to do with that stupid development project. He's just the accountant on it, but he's thrown himself into it heart and soul. He's been talking about nothing else."

"That's understandable, I guess," Linda said. "He's related to the Reynolds, isn't he?"

She nodded. "He's a distant cousin. I don't know why he's so keen on the story. It's awful."

On the wrap-around porch, the two men tried the front door, then some of the windows before moving toward the back of the house.

"Is it one of those unsolved mystery things?" Linda asked.

"No, not at all. Twenty-five years ago, around Christmas time, in front of a houseful of guests, Charles Reynolds knifed his pregnant wife, then drowned himself in the river. It was a senseless tragedy that nearly destroyed the Reynolds family. It's not," Susan said firmly, "something to laugh off."

"Why did Charles do it?"

"They said he thought that his wife was cheating on him, that the baby wasn't his own. They call it the Othello Affair because it wasn't true; she was faithful."

Linda tapped her chin thoughtfully. "There has to be more to it than that. Lots of women cheat on their husbands and the husbands don't all go crazy and kill people."

Susan hesitated and Linda knew she was not telling all of it.

"What else, Susan?"

At that moment, Michael reappeared on the porch, waving them in.

13

"Come on!" he called.

To Linda's surprise, Susan immediately opened the door and began trudging through the snow towards her husband.

She watched her friend make her careful way up to the porch and thought, *What on earth could be so terrible about this case that she wouldn't want to tell me?*

"Linda!"

Michael was waving for her, too. Rather than be left behind in the car, Linda got out and joined them.

CHAPTER 3

Michael recognized Susan's unhappiness as she came up the steps to join him. He took her gloved hand and gave it a sympathetic squeeze.

"Johnny found a way in." He lowered his voice. "Just a quick look around, sweetheart, then we'll go, I promise."

When she looked up at him, her solemn expression marred with worry, he could think of nothing reassuring to say. He knew his wife did not like his recent pre-occupation with the Reynolds murder, but he could not help himself – there was something about the story that drew his attention and absorbed him in a way that nothing else ever had. He had become the resident expert on the case in the office to the obvious discomfort of his colleagues, many of whom found his fascination to be tasteless and a possible deterrent to his advancement within the company. This detour was more than a pilgrimage to a site of family interest. Michael was convinced that if he could just see River House before it was torn down he could get the Reynolds murder-suicide out of his system for good.

Standing here, in the shadow of the house that he had read so much about, he was sure that he was right. However, he could not explain all of this to Susan, not with Linda standing only a foot away. So he smiled, brushed a quick kiss on her cheek and then led them around the porch to where Johnny was waiting.

"You'll like this place, Linda," he called out as they walked. "It's a sturdy old house, built in the 1880s by the Venerable Josiah Reynolds, esquire. Lots of history here."

"I'm a nurse, Michael, not a historian," she quipped and he laughed as they drew around the corner.

Johnny stood, arms folded, staring out at the broad expanse of river, his expression inscrutable. He was at the head of the stairs, where the generous porch led out onto a snow covered patio. Michael knew from his familiarity with the house's blueprints that there was a path and a staircase leading down to the old boat house and the infamous dock from which Charles Reynolds had thrown himself into the river in a fit of mad repentance.

The old boat house, battered and worn with time, was large and still showed evidence of the scallop trim and peeling brown paint matching the somber house above. Unlike River House, however, the boat house had been breached; a rotted old pine had crushed the roof, leaving only three walls to sag in final defiance.

Regardless of what happens to River House, Michael thought, *the boat house would have to come down. But the dock looks as sturdy as if it were only a few years old.*

Johnny did not seem to notice their approach until Linda came up to his side and nodded at the dock.

"I guess that's where it happened, huh?" She shoved her hands deeper into her coat.

16

Johnny looked startled.

"I guess," he said, and turned away. He stepped past Susan and wrenched open the back door. "Let's get inside before we freeze."

As Johnny disappeared through the doorway, Susan shot Michael a concerned look. The wind toyed with her hair and sent threads of ice through Michael's clothing. He shivered and gestured towards the house.

"Come on," he said.

Linda followed her brother, burying her chin into the thick collar of her coat. Susan looked around as though seeking an excuse not to enter. The wind whistled through the tree tops. At the sound, she lunged for the doorway. Michael followed her, shutting the door behind him.

The room spread out before them vast and cavernous. Inside was not appreciably warmer, but they were at least sheltered from the wind. Michael unbuttoned his top button gratefully and looked around.

"What a *room!*" Linda exclaimed. She stood in the middle, turning in a slow circle. "It's *huge.*"

This back room took up nearly the entire rear half of the house. The wall facing the river was lined with long windows, each with its own window seat, and two sets of French double doors. The windows were all still intact, courtesy of the shutters, which remained mostly shut. Some, weakened by wind, time, and wear, flapped open to allow light to pour in. An enormous fireplace dominated the wall facing opposite the windows. The floor was parquet, worn and warped in spots, but still gleaming. A chandelier, shrouded in cobwebs and dust, clinked with the unexpected movement of air. A grand piano, draped with a dust cloth, sat in a place of honor in one corner of the ballroom.

River House, Michael knew, had been built to impress. Despite twenty years of neglect, the room still performed.

"Amazing." Linda shook her head, whistling in admiration.

Johnny wandered around the edges of the room, his hands jammed in his pockets, warily scanning the walls and furnishings.

"It's in good condition," Susan said, her voice sounding stronger and more relaxed. She had been unusually touchy all day and on the brink of car-sickness the entire trip. Caught up in this moment of exploring, she looked more like herself.

Maybe she just needed to get out of the car, Michael thought.

"It's still beautiful," Susan continued. "In a creepy, rundown way, I mean."

"It is," Michael agreed, looking around himself. "It'd be a crime to tear this down."

"Why, Michael!" Johnny grinned. "Such disloyalty. What *would* Mr. North say?"

Linda, meanwhile, had found the light switches and pressed a few, but nothing happened.

"I don't suppose anyone brought a flashlight?" she asked.

"I wasn't expecting to go house hunting," Johnny returned.

Michael, who had been a Boy Scout, fished his pocket lamp out of his jacket and turned it on. The stream of light was sharp and bright. Even so, it seemed weak compared to the gloom that threatened to overwhelm even the bright sunshine pouring through the windows.

"Always prepared," Michael said and was rewarded with a grin from Susan. She went over and tucked her arm through his.

"It is kind of exciting," she whispered to him. "Like being a kid again."

Susan always seemed pretty to Michael. She had that girl-next-door look with a touch of majesty in her short stature and absolutely the best taste in clothing that he had ever seen in a girl. She had been called 'The Queen' on campus, but it was her kind heart and gorgeous smile that had first drawn him in. Even at her most disheveled, Susan was always appealing to him. But at that moment, peering up at him through the half-light, her eyes aglow with a sudden return of confidence and unusual mischievousness, she looked more than pretty – she was radiantly beautiful.

"We aren't just going to stay in here, are we?" Linda's voice sliced through the fragile moment. "I thought someone promised me ghosts."

"Well, if its ghosts you want," Johnny reached the double doors leading out of the room and threw them open with a jerk. "Let's go and find some!"

If it was dim in the ballroom, the entryway beyond was a black hole, absorbing what little light illuminated the foursome. Even Johnny, who had seemed prepared to charge into anything, hesitated at the edge of the darkness.

There was a hissing noise. Susan gasped, but it was only Linda, sucking air through her teeth.

"If there were any such things as ghosts," Susan whispered. "They'd be in there, all right."

Then Linda said, in a stilted tone, "It's weird. It's like... I can almost hear Christmas music."

Johnny snorted and turned. "For a woman of science, you sure spook easily."

Johnny's figure in the doorway reminded Michael of something. He pointed the flashlight just over Johnny's shoulder, causing the soldier to flinch and look at him in askance.

"It was right there," Michael said. He had not meant to whisper. With effort, he cleared his throat and spoke normally.

"Right there is where Charles Reynolds came into the party that night, exactly at midnight, twenty-five years ago."

Susan squeezed his arm. Linda and Johnny were looking at Michael with such interest that he was encouraged to go on. He let go of Susan and went to stand next to Johnny. Outside, the wind sung about the eaves, trees bobbing under its influence. The room seemed to come alive with their dancing shadows.

"Right here," Michael continued, raising his voice to be heard about the increasing noise. He turned to face the two women. "Imagine: the room is filled with light and sound. A small band plays. Servants pass around drinks while elegant people in diamonds and silks dance. The war is over. It's 1946 and everyone is still celebrating. Suddenly, in comes Charles Reynolds, wearing a blood-spattered coat and no tie."

Johnny stepped away from the door and moved back towards the windows, rubbing his shoulders as though feeling a draft. Michael barely noticed. He had become wrapped in the details of the story and the tale rolled out of him without encouragement.

"He's just come down from his wife's room. He's gray, panicked, agitated - he doesn't quite understand what's happened. His nightmares are mixing with reality and he can't distinguish one from the other anymore. In his confusion, he still has the razor - his wife's Christmas gift to him, an old fashioned thing with a long wooden handle. His initials are carved in it, pressing against his palm. It's dripping with Helene's blood when he enters the ballroom. Someone screams and everyone stops, horrified. Charles is confused, then he realizes what he has done. He has killed the woman he loves. It's a crime. He decides then and there that punishment must be severe and irrevocable. With an unearthly cry, he lifts the razor… and runs through the terrified crowd to the dock, the river, and his own destruction."

As though on cue, the wind caught one of the rotting shutters and slammed it against the window near to Johnny, making him jump. Linda shrieked involuntarily. Michael came to with a start and realized, with a sort of shock, that he had taken a few unconscious steps forward, lifting his hand into the air in imitation of the long-dead man.

Linda pressed a hand to her beating heart and then looked at Johnny. He stood frozen at the window, staring at the quivering shutter that cut off his view of the river and dock. Even in the dim light, they could see his fists were clenched. Only Susan, standing silently where Michael had left her, seemed unaffected.

"Really, Michael," she said patiently. "Isn't it a little early for spooky tales?"

Her practical question broke the uneasy spell and Linda laughed in relief.

"I'll say," she said. "I think you've missed your calling, Mikey. You ought to write for the Alfred Hitchcock Magazine."

Michael chuckled uncomfortably. It was not like him to be so dramatic and he was embarrassed.

"This place certainly has atmosphere," he said.

Linda responded with an enthusiastic, "It sure does! Reminds me of those creepy old Nancy Drew novels I used to read. Anyone want to explore?"

"Not without another flashlight," Susan said. "Look, Michael, yours is dying."

She was right. Already the beam was losing its battle against the shadows which were gathering at an astonishing rate. Michael looked out one of the open windows. The sky, which had been blue with some clouds before, was now a solid ceiling of steel-gray.

This doesn't make sense, Michael thought. *The storm isn't supposed to hit until around ten...and I put fresh batteries in this before I left the house.*

"The storm's coming in quickly." Johnny said. His tone was flat, emotionless. "We ought to leave now."

"Not yet!" Linda cried. She was peering into the darkened entryway with childlike interest. "Ten minutes more won't make a difference. Don't you have another flashlight, Michael?"

"In the glove compartment," Michael said.

Johnny said sharply, "I'll get it."

"Oh, good!" Linda said.

When Johnny returned, stomping the snow off of his boots and shaking flakes out of his hair, he looked grim.

"It's getting bad out," he reported. "How much farther to Susan's place?"

"An hour," Susan said.

Michael said, "The storm can't be that far along. We've got hours yet, according to the weather bureau."

"We ought to go now." Johnny handed Michael the heavy flashlight. "Before it gets worse."

Michael was about to protest when Susan laid her hand on his arm.

"Please, Michael," she said. "I don't want to be caught in a snow storm."

The wind roared as if to second her motion. Something slammed against the roof above them. This time even Susan jumped.

Linda chirped in fright and hurried over to the rest of the group. "Okay, okay," she said. "That's enough for me. Let's go before we get stuck here all night."

With that the matter was settled. They filed out into the gathering storm.

Michael was the last to leave. He stole a lingering glance behind him before he stepped out. The room lay silent and still. Nothing breathed, nothing moved, nothing bid him stay. Yet, as he shut the door, he could not help but feel as though he was leaving someone behind.

CHAPTER 4

There was in the air a sense of impending battle. Johnny knew it like he knew the scent of napalm. The world was conspiring against them, gathering forces, preparing to strike. The wind was the first line, whipping up the light snow from the ground and sending it, stinging, into their faces as they struggled through the drifts towards the car. Johnny took the lead and Michael brought up the rear. It was not snowing yet, but Johnny could taste it in the air and he did not like it. The storm was moving much too fast.

He pulled open the passenger door and helped Linda in while Susan moved around the front of the vehicle towards her door. Michael stumbled next to him, fumbling for the handle.

"You're right," he said to Johnny, raising his voice to be heard above the wind. "Let's get out of here before a tree falls."

There was an audible sigh of relief when the doors were shut. After turning over twice, the engine started. Michael shifted into reverse and pulled backwards as the wind, roaring in defeat, slammed into the side of the car, causing the entire vehicle to shudder.

"Good grief!" Linda said. "What is with the weather today?"

No one answered her. Michael had gone too deep into the drifts behind them and was gently trying to ease the spinning tires back onto pavement. Susan looked ill again. Johnny found himself sitting at attention as though expecting an attack at any minute.

Stop it, he told himself, and then said aloud to Linda, "It's just the wind coming off the river, that's all. Want me to get out and push, Mike?"

Even as he said it, the tires caught traction and they began moving towards the road.

"We're on our way now," Michael said heartily. "Just a little bit of New England weather."

His white knuckle-hold on the constantly shifting steering wheel belied his confident tone. They knew better than to reply. Even the backseat passengers could feel the shift of the slipping tires while they were still on flat ground. All around them, the wind whipped up the sugar-like snow, casting drifts and fresh layers onto their path.

The driveway was only a few hundred yards long, ending in a sharp downslope to the road. Michael slowed as he reached it, until the tires caught ground and held.

"It's slippery," Susan warned.

Michael said, "I know, honey, I know," as he eased the car forward. They reached the lip of the incline and the car tipped.

"Easy does it..." Michael said, just before the tires touched ice.

The car hurtled down the slope, picking up speed and twisting as Michael fought for control. Johnny braced himself and reached out for Linda, who had one hand clasped to her mouth. Susan was climbing up into her seat, bracing her legs against the dashboard, repeatedly crying, "Michael, the tree! Michael, the *tree!*"

The car turned despite Michael's frantic struggle with the wheel and pounding on the brakes. They slipped down the end of the driveway, slid across the road and tipped over the edge into the ditch. Susan's scream was cut off abruptly when they hit the trees with a crescendo of breaking glass and the bone-crunching sound of metal wrapping around wood.

CHAPTER 5

I t took them some time to get Johnny out. He was buried in gifts, containers, and sleeping bags. When he was finally free from the car, they paused to survey the damage. The wind had calmed a little but the cold remained, icing through their clothes as they shivered and pressed handkerchiefs to foreheads.

Personal damage was mercifully minimal. Linda was shaken and bruised from the boxes she had landed on. The two men sitting on the driver's side, which had smashed up against the tree, were bruised and they sported some shallow cuts from the flying glass. Michael's arm was hurting too, but he brushed it off.

Susan, who had suffered the least, was as close as she had ever come to hysterics. The sobs she muffled into her hand choked her throat. She alternated between checking Michael, running a hand on his bleeding face, and stumbling off by herself, bent over. It was so unlike his usually sturdy, reliable wife, the one who had worked two years in the emergency room, that Michael did not know what to do. After tending to her brother, Linda stepped in. Pulling a blanket out of the car, she wrapped it around her friend's shoulders, sat her on a stump a few feet away, and made her breathe. With the two women occupied, Michael turned back to the car. Johnny was already there, reaching into the backseat.

Michael gestured helplessly at the wreck. "Do you think we can pull it out?"

Johnny shot him a look and stepped back, pulling his duffel bag out with him. "No way," he said. "Even if you and I could peel it off of the tree, you can't drive it in that condition."

Michael had already known this; he simply did not want to acknowledge it. Of everyone in the group, he knew best what a tight spot they were in.

"Shoot," he said.

"Yeah." Johnny nodded. "So, what do we do now? Walk to the neighbors?"

"We can't." Michael had to raise his voice over the sudden gust of wind which shook the snow out of the branches. "There isn't another house for at least three miles, and most of them are summer places. No heat, no hot water, and no phone. Besides," he nodded towards where Susan and Linda were huddled, "I can't ask her to walk in this weather."

Johnny hitched up his duffel bag and looked back at where they had come from. "They won't like staying there."

"Neither will I," Michael said.

They walked over to the women. As they approached, Susan pulled herself up, tossed her hair out of her eyes and brushed Linda's reassuring hand off of her shoulder. When Michael reached for her, she rose and said, "We aren't going anywhere, are we?"

Michael shook his head. "Not in that car."

Linda swore as Johnny said, "We have to find shelter. Michael thought there was a place about three miles back, but…"

Susan interrupted, "That's too far." Her face was tearstained but her tone was steady and her eyes were firm. "We can stay in the Reynolds place." She fixed her eyes on Michael. "We'll be safe there."

They all stared at her. The wind made the trees rustle violently and Michael thought the day had grown a shade darker.

"There's no reason why we shouldn't," Johnny said.

By his tone, Michael knew that Johnny was wondering why he was hesitating. Michael looked over Susan's shoulder and saw that Linda was biting her lip. She was thinking the same thing he was. Neither believed in ghosts, but everyone knew that Johnny was a haunted man. Being isolated in such a place having the history that he did seemed risky. Then there was Susan, who had been running hot and cold all day, hysterical one minute and calmly resolute the next.

I should take her to the hospital, Michael thought and his teeth ground. *But there's no way to get there until tomorrow at least. I could make it in this storm, but I can't ask her…*

The wind roared and Michael found himself saying, "Let's get everything we need out of the car before it's buried."

The decision was made.

CHAPTER 6

Linda insisted that Susan should be left in the house while the others brought in what they could from the car.

"You're in shock," she said. "You need to be out of the elements."

The men agreed, and though Susan insisted on carrying something, she did not argue the decision. She knew she was not in shock — it was worse than that — but both she and Linda had been in the medical field long enough to know the dangers of self-diagnosis. Besides, they all needed medical treatment and Susan could set that up while the others brought in the supplies.

I will not crumble when they need me, she thought determinedly. *I will not.*

Linda and Johnny escorted her in, leaving Michael to unload the car. Johnny had the larger flashlight and walked quickly through the ballroom, as though he were trying to avoid it. They found themselves in the entryway with a living room on one side and the dining room on the other. Just beyond the dining room was the kitchen, a huge, cavernous place almost institutional in its size and starkness. The dining room, like the ballroom, was sparsely furnished with a battered table and some fragile antique chairs. There was nothing on the walls or on the Victorian sideboard. The room had the look, Susan thought, of being picked over by someone who was limited by the space of a moving van.

Johnny dumped his duffel on the table and propped the flashlight up next to it to illuminate the room.

"I'll help Michael," he said. "See if you can find some candles, Lin."

"Let me help you guys first," Linda said, then turned, half-apologetic to Susan. "Will you be all right in here by yourself?"

Johnny paused in the doorway to wait for her response.

Susan was surprised at them. She was a grown woman after all and no longer afraid of the dark. She wondered, *Why do I feel so comfortable here?*

"I'm fine," she assured them. "I was just shaken up outside, that's all. I'm not an invalid."

Linda frowned and Johnny said, "Let us handle it, Lin. You find candles. There have to be some, probably in the kitchen."

"Right."

He left, but Linda did not move to look around. Instead, she waited until the clomping sound of Johnny's boots disappeared into the frigid outdoors. Then she went over to where Susan sat and knelt at her feet, looking up into her shadowed face. She took her hand and squeezed it.

"How far along are you?" Linda asked.

Susan's breath caught. Her free hand went to her stomach and her strange calm deserted her in a flutter of anxiety. The accident, the impact had driven her knees into her stomach. Her abdominal muscles were sore and fear made her legs weak and her eyes water.

"Two months," she whispered, her voice quavering.

31

Linda's grip tightened on her hand. "Does Michael know?"

"No. It was going to be a surprise for Christmas. Oh, Linda, what if...?"

"Hush," Linda said in a firm, no-nonsense tone. It melted immediately into concern. "Susan, we can't know for certain, you know that."

Susan squeezed her eyes shut. "But the baby's so small," she whispered.

"I'm sure it's fine, Susan. Women are strong, right? Pioneer women used to wrangle horses and chop wood in the morning before giving birth in the afternoon. I'm sure it's fine. I'm sure."

Linda sounded anything but sure and Susan knew that she had no right to be. She sank down into the chair, into herself, and buried her face in her free hand. How could this happen? Everything had been going so smoothly, so according to plan. She had married Michael, set up house with him, worked her job as a good modern woman should. She was a competent nurse who resisted the advances of lecherous doctors and always kept her calm and composure. Her mother even told her she was proud of her, a rare, hard-earned compliment.

Now this.

How could I have allowed this to happen?

What if she had lost the baby? How could she live with losing Michael's child? How could he live with knowing he had been the inadvertent cause? This Christmas was their first as man and wife. Would it become the anniversary of a tragedy?

Michael doesn't have to know, she thought. *I don't have to tell him I was ever pregnant.*

But she would tell him. They had always been honest with each other and this secret was too big for her to carry alone. He would have to know and in knowing, realize his responsibility.

Then they would have to live with it. She choked back another sob.

I haven't even held it yet. How can I miss someone so much whom I haven't even met and have only known about for a few weeks?

"Susan, we don't know that anything's wrong yet. It could be all right."

Linda's voice sounded so far away. Suddenly, Susan wished she was a child again, that she could talk to her grandmother again. Grandmother Louise had such a soothing way about her —unlike Susan's mother, Grandmother Louise cared nothing for 'show and the spectacle', as she used to say.

"We need messes and bruises in the world, just as much as we need poise and calm, Susan. You aren't a robot and thank God for it!"

There was no tragedy that she could not smooth out into a minor triumph, if only of character. She would hold Susan in her lap and stroke her forehead with her cool hand, the scent of her lilac soap wrapping little Susan like a hug...

There was a whisper in the room, a breath of air like a draft. Linda stiffened, but Susan, lost in her memories, stayed perfectly still. A feeling, like a warm, soft wind, swept over Susan. She could almost feel her grandmother's presence reassuring her. She was fine. The baby would be fine. They were all fine. There was warmth in the room, means of comfort. They would find light, there would be food, and they could wait out the storm in safety. They would all be protected, guarded, and safe. Funny, she could almost smell her grandmother's cinnamon coffee cake...

As suddenly as the feeling came, it went, and Susan became aware of Linda's cold hand, the dark, hollow room, the flashlight's small beam, the isolation of the house, and her own sore abdomen. Suddenly she felt embarrassed. She was religious, but sensible. This sort of thing was not what sensible girls believed in.

Fairy tales, she told herself sternly.

Linda's words sliced through the fog of confusion: "We should tell Michael."

Susan sat up sharply. In the distance, they heard the voices of the two men, returning to the house with a load of luggage. Linda made a small sound and Susan realized that she was still squeezing her friend's hand. She loosened her hold and bent over she was until within inches of Linda's face.

"*No,*" she whispered fiercely. "Don't tell him anything. The last thing I want is for him to worry and feel guilty about an accident that wasn't his fault. Please, Linda," she pleaded as the men drew near. "Please, don't tell him."

Linda hesitated, clearly torn. The men entered the room then, stomping off snow, arms burdened with supplies. She nodded acquiescence and stood up, pulling her hands out of Susan's.

Susan let go a deep breath.

Please, God, she prayed. *Please, God, let everything be all right.*

"One more load," Michael said, his jovial tone a poor mask for the concern he clearly felt. "Feeling better, honey?"

"She's fine," Linda said calmly. "But I'll feel better once we all get checked out thoroughly. You shouldn't be carrying things with that arm, you know."

Michael argued that he was fine and Johnny concurred.

Linda folded her arms. "Typical," she snorted. "All men think they're John Wayne."

"If John Wayne was here," Michael said, "he'd be asking for *our* autograph."

Linda threw her hat at them as they left, laughing.

34

She turned back to Susan. In the half-light, Linda looked older and Susan suddenly remembered their age gap.

"Are you all right?" Linda asked.

Susan nodded. The atmosphere of comfort had evaporated but it had taken with it her crippling fear and anxiety. She felt strangely at peace. She could not explain it, but under the circumstances she was not going to risk questioning it either.

"I'm fine," she said and stood. "Let's find those candles."

CHAPTER 7

Emptying the car took more trips than Johnny and Michael had originally planned. Susan told them to bring in the foodstuffs as well.

"It was intended for the Christmas party," she said. "But under the circumstances, I don't think Mom will mind."

Her swift change from being the victim to being in command worried Michael and he mentioned this to Johnny as they trudged back to the car for the third time. Johnny thought her behavior was perfectly normal.

"Once the brain accepts that no amount of pouting or crying can change a situation, the other instincts kick in," he said, hopping into the car before Michael could volunteer. "For some people, they become the victim and despair. For people like Susan, they face the situation and start taking charge. It's nothing to worry about. She's a strong woman."

"You've seen this on the battlefront?" Michael asked.

Johnny clenched his teeth instinctively. Michael was a great guy, almost like a brother, but he was occasionally tactless. Johnny did not feel like delving into his recent past or current struggle, but he answered anyway. He, like Susan, preferred to face the situation as soon as it arrived,

"Yeah," he said, "a couple of times."

To stop any further inquiry, Johnny threw an armload of afghans at Michael.

After everything was out of the car, they rigged up a flag made out of one of Michael's red mittens, some string, and the radio antennae. Johnny bent the antennae so that it hung out more conspicuously over the road while Michael wrote a quick note in bold letters and tucked it into the dashboard.

"Just in case someone comes along," he shouted over the wind. His lips were blue and his teeth were chattering. "Let's get inside."

Johnny nodded and followed, thinking, *No one's going to see that sign. No one is even going to see the car. We are alone up here.*

It was not a happy thought.

Inside, the girls had found candles and candlesticks in the kitchen cabinets. They were busily setting up in the dining room. Johnny suggested that they look at the heating system to see if they could get it started. Michael enthusiastically agreed, but the two nurses were adamant that everyone be treated first.

"You won't be able to do much without light and water," Johnny pointed out.

"We have light," Linda said.

"And we can melt snow," Susan replied.

"How?" Michael asked, making a show of rubbing his arms and shivering. "Holding a pan over the candlelight?"

"Hardee har har," Linda said. "It'll be a few minutes then, wise guys."

"Fine," Johnny said. "Let us know when it's ready. Come on, Michael, let's start looking."

They found the furnace in short order. It was an oil heater and it quickly became apparent that they would not be able to use it tonight.

"I guess it's time to start looking for wood," Michael said.

Johnny nodded, but said nothing. The basement was roughly finished, with a low ceiling that brushed his head as he moved.

"This was where some of the servants worked back in the good old days," Michael said. "Look, there's an old laundry machine." The beam from his flashlight lit up an antique that Johnny would not have been able to identify. "My grandmother had one like it. Imagine working your whole life in a place like this?"

"Cheerful working conditions," he commented. He nearly completed the thought with, *I've had worse*, but stopped himself. This was not the time and, besides, Johnny was not a bleeding heart. Not yet, anyway, though he wondered how much more of this house he could take. There were cobwebs hanging down from the basement ceiling, touching their hands and faces as they moved, reminding him uncomfortably of other times he had been in the dark and frightened. A cold draft washed over them, and Johnny shivered.

Pull it together, Vincent.

It was not the shadows that frightened him, but the memories. They clung to his conscious like gremlins, always present, but just out of sight, undefeatable, untouchable, his own private 'Nam. He managed to stay sane, but only just and that was thanks to therapy, pills, and sheer determination. Staying in this house with its creaks, groans, and bitter memories would test him, but he would not crumble. Not again. Not when Linda and the others were depending on him.

It's just an old house with creaks and groans. Keep it together.

"Let's go then," he said. He turned, took a few steps forward and then froze. A long moan cut through the silence like a knife, setting his nerves on edge. It came from somewhere above them, high above, an unearthly sound that was far too low to be one of the women. His hand instinctively reached for his left hip – but he was not in the jungle and his gun was no longer there. He looked behind him and jumped.

Michael had turned the flashlight on himself, making faces in the sharp beam. His features were grotesquely shadowed and for a moment, the briefest, most frightening moment, he did not look like Michael at all, but something fiendish.

Michael laughed and the moment shattered.

"Don't do that," Johnny scolded.

Michael pointed the light away. "It *is* creepy in here," he said. Now his face was so dark that Johnny could not see the movement of his mouth. "That wind sounded like the death throes of a ghost. You could almost believe in them in this house, couldn't you?"

The moan had faded away, taking the draft with it. Overhead, he could faintly hear the sound of Linda's laughter. It strengthened his resolve.

"Ghosts are already dead," Johnny said, firmly. "I don't believe in them anyway. Come on, Michael. Let's find something to burn."

CHAPTER 8

Linda and Susan had agreed that if they were going to stay overnight, they might as well enjoy themselves. Neither said it openly, but each was grimly determined to avoid talking about the big concern.

"I brought wine," Linda said, cheerily pulling out two bottles of cheap chardonnay from her bag. "I would have brought beer, but I was trying to impress your folks."

"If you had, you would have won over my dad," Susan replied, as she sorted through the appetizers that were to be their dinner. "He's the salt of the earth."

"Susan!" Michael called. "We're going to look for wood for a fire. You two all right?"

"No razor-wielding wackos yet," Linda said. "But we'll keep you informed."

The two men went outside and Linda turned to Susan, "We can do this later, Susie. Let's take a look around the place. It's not often I'm a house guest of one of the wealthiest firms in Boston. Plus, if we move fast, we can pick our rooms before the boys do."

That seemed a worthwhile enterprise, so Susan took a candle and followed her out of the dining room.

The main floor where they stood was divided into two parts: the ballroom, which took up almost the entirety of the back of the house, and the front rooms, which were divided by the entryway. On one side were the kitchen and the dining room, with stairs leading down into the basement. In the entryway, a broad staircase swept to the second floor landing, providing a suitable showcase for the lady of the house's grand entrance.

"Can't you picture Scarlett O'Hara coming down in her grand ball gown?" Linda asked.

"In a Yankee's house? She'd rather die!"

They crossed the entryway and entered the stately living room. It had high ceilings and shadowed squares on the walls where paintings must have hung. Only a few pieces of cloth covered furniture remained. Susan toyed with the idea of uncovering some pieces, but Linda charged on to the door on the far side and opened it.

"I believe we have found the study," she declared. "Ooo, you'll like this room, Susan! Look at all the books!"

Susan followed her. Three steps led down into a long, narrow room, lined with built-in bookshelves and large shuttered windows. At the far end overlooking the front drive, a massive wooden desk stood, denuded of paraphernalia and without a chair. A shrouded couch stood in the middle of the room flanked by magazine holders. The carpet, once green, was now gray with dust. Those walls which were not covered in bookshelves were papered in peeling brown and white. An air of quiet detachment prevailed. Clearly, this was supposed to be a sanctuary space.

"What a magnificent old desk!" Linda said. She hopped down the stairs and went over to inspect it. "This looks like the dean's desk, doesn't it? I wonder what it's made of. It probably cost more than I make in a year."

Susan stepped farther inside and craned her neck to look at the shelves, some open, others glass encased. Though there were large gaps where the more valuable tomes of the collection had been removed, there were still enough left to keep a reader busy for days. A battered but matching collection of Scott's novels claimed one shelf, while the Encyclopedia Britannica, two decades out of date, took two shelves. There were other groupings, some with matching bindings, others which were unmatched. They stood or lay where the movers had left them, interspaced with some bric-a-brac that was too little valued to be stored.

"At least we'll have plenty to read," Susan said.

Linda grunted as she began pulling desk drawers open. "Bet you won't find one Ellery Queen or Nero Wolfe in the bunch."

"You have to broaden your reading," Susan teased, running her hand along one line of books. "A little Sir Walter Scott wouldn't hurt you."

She bent over to examine a set of about fifteen little black books, each the size of Susan's hand. The gilt lettering on their spines was so worn that it could no longer be read. Still, something had caught her eye, so she pulled one out, opening it to the title page: *The Tragedy of Othello.*

Susan shut it quickly, shivering.

Of all the books to pick up...

She shoved it back into place, fighting back the idea that its pages would be bloodstained.

"I've found the Reynolds' family Shakespeare collection," she said aloud. She looked at Linda and frowned. "Isn't that a little invasive, going through someone else's drawers?"

Linda was bent over the desk, leafing through large yellowing magazines. She shrugged. "No one's lived here in ten years. If there was anything they wanted protected, they would have taken it with them. Besides, except for these gossip magazines, they're all empty so far..." She pulled open the last drawer and grunted, "Bingo." Then, in a softer, awed tone, she muttered, "Gosh."

"What is it?"

She pulled out a small stack of newspapers, files, and a decaying photo album. She dropped them on the desktop as Susan stepped forward for a closer look.

"I think I've just discovered Rachel Reynolds' files on the Othello case," Linda said.

CHAPTER 9

There was no firewood in the house, nor was there any around the edges of the building. Johnny suggested that they might use some of the furniture for kindling, but Michael baulked at the idea.

"It's not ours to burn," he pointed out.

"It's going to get awfully cold tonight," Johnny insisted. He stomped his feet and the tread made a hollow sound on the boards. "I didn't bring an ax to use on the trees."

Michael sighed and looked around. They were standing on the porch, having already trekked all the way around the building. The wind was picking up again, howling like a banshee over the swaying pine trees and sending the light snow whirling across the patio. It was not yet five and the temperature was dropping rapidly. Michael did not want to stay outside any longer than was absolutely necessary. Johnny was right. They had to burn something.

He scanned the backyard and his eyes fell on the sagging boathouse.

"Let's use that," he suggested, gesturing towards it.

Johnny turned and his expression of mild annoyance faded to ambiguity when he fastened his eyes on it. Had Michael been looking, he would have seen the other man's face turn ghostly white above the black scarf he wore around his neck.

Michael did not see. Seized with a sudden feeling of usefulness, he had gone charging down the staircase and into the shifting snow scape below.

"Let's gather as much as we can before the storm hits," he called over his shoulder. He plunged through drifts that varied in height from ankle to knee deep and laughed when he saw Johnny still standing on the porch, staring. "Hey, Captain America! Since you aren't too keen on slogging through the snow, why don't you take that shovel behind you and dig us a path while I start breaking up some lumber?"

Johnny turned slowly. He took the rusted shovel that had been left by the door, and walked down the porch stairs with all the eagerness of a man walking to his own hanging. Once his feet touched snow, however, his attitude changed.

He called out to Michael, already half way to the boathouse, "Ten bucks says I'll meet you there, Bucky!"

Michael's laughter drifted over the wind.

CHAPTER 10

Susan did not want to go through the files that Linda had found.

"I feel like Michael's talked about the whole thing so much, I know the story by heart," she said, viewing Linda's find with distaste. "Any further reading will give me even more nightmares than I expect to have in this spooky place. I want to finish exploring. I won't sleep well until I've seen everything."

Linda was disappointed by Susan's lack of interest. However, though she was too sensible to believe in ghosts, she knew that she would sleep better knowing that there was no one else in the house. Carrying Rachel's research, she followed Susan out of the library, through the living room, and into the entryway, where she dumped the pile on a dusty hall table.

"There," she said. "Now, let's go explore."

The staircase went up to a landing overlooking the entryway through elegantly carved wooden railings. Linda paused at the banisters, looking out over the room below. The parquet flooring looked like modernistic art. The chandelier, threaded with cobwebs and coated in dust, shifted gently on its chain.

Shame, she thought. *All this grandeur lost and forgotten.*

"What are you looking at?" Susan asked.

"Just the view. I was trying to think…didn't Michael say that Irene North died here a few years ago, slipping down the stairs?"

Susan shivered. "Yes."

Linda ran her hand along the railing, feeling the smooth polish beneath. "I wonder if it were these stairs or the others…"

"It was this staircase," Susan said firmly. When Linda turned to look at her, she gestured. "Come on, let's explore."

The second floor was divided into two wings, right and left. Susan went immediately to the left and Linda followed.

They found five doors, three on their left, and two on their right. Linda opened the first door to their right and stuck her head in.

"Bedroom," she declared. "Oh, with a bathroom."

She stepped in and Susan followed. The room was long, with bay windows looking out to the river and mountains, or would have, had they not been shuttered. It was empty, with only a closet, a radiator, and the windows to break the monotony of the mint green walls.

The bathroom was small but comfortable, with a claw-foot bath and a tri-fold mirror above the sink. It had two doors, one opening into the hall and the other into the next bedroom. This bedroom was bigger than the first with a long, shallow closet and scars on the walls where pictures once hung.

"Wouldn't mind having a shack like this to call home," Linda said. "Still, it's a little underwhelming for millionaires, don't you think?"

"This was their summer place," Susan said. "I suppose they were trying to keep it simple."

"I guess." Linda stroked the elaborate wainscoting. "But then again, would you look at the detail in this place?" She pulled her hand away, black with dust and grime. "Too bad they let the maid go."

The door on the left side of the hallway revealed another empty room very much like the others. When they came to the final room in that wing, both women stopped short. Unlike the other rooms in the house, which were either empty or sparsely furnished, this bedroom looked as though the owners had left one morning and simply forgotten to come back.

This room was rectangular, with shuttered bay windows on two walls, one overlooking the drive. The dust-covered curtains were pulled back in their catches as though to let the sun in. A door, slightly ajar, led to the small bathroom on their right.

The furniture was matched, early American style, heavy and well made. An enormous four-poster bed faced the windows. The mattress was bare, with only a few tired, case-less pillows piled on top. On the other side of the bed was a side table and beyond that was a closet. Scattered about the room were a bureau, an armchair resting by a fireplace, and a vanity under its own light fixture. A desk with a matching chair sat under one of the windows. There were pictures and paintings on the walls and personal items scattered about; a pen set and writing mat on the desk, a brush set and perfume bottles on the vanity, an alarm clock on the table next to the bed. A blanket lay where someone carelessly tossed it on the armchair.

Susan and Linda stepped inside. The carpet under their feet was thick, muffling the sound of their steps.

"It seems warmer in here somehow," Susan said.

Linda nodded, but she shivered anyway. "Feels like Rachel is coming back at any moment."

She went to the vanity and examined the items. There was a matching brush, comb, and hand-held mirror, some perfume bottles, and a compact that looked at least a decade old. The brush set looked even older.

Poor Rachel, she thought. *I wonder if she wanted to go to Florida or if it was a family decision. But why would she leave her necessities behind?*

As she ran through other possible explanations, a sickly-sweet sound filled the silent void. Something was playing *'I'll be Home for Christmas.'* She turned sharply, her heart pounding.

Susan was on the other side of the bed, standing by the window with her hand on the back of the armchair. She had a pensive expression on her face, thrown into sharper relief due to the candle she held. She did not seem disturbed by the sound of the music, which Linda could still hear, a tinkling sound, like a music box.

It took her a second before she realized that Susan was watching a carved wooden box on the side table. Two figures, a man in black and a woman in ghostly white, twirled in fits and starts as the old mechanics struggled to keep in time.

Susan saw her staring and shook herself, as though waking from a dream. "It's an old music box. Isn't it pretty?"

The figures pirouetted one last time before grinding to a halt, mid-chorus. Susan leaned over, but rather than wind it again, she carefully shut the lid. Linda was relieved. The sound was too sweet, like an echo of a memory or a shade of a past event best forgotten.

She must have had this thought reflected in her expression because when Susan turned, she frowned. "What is it, Linda?"

Not wanting to admit that she had been unnerved by a child's plaything, Linda gestured around the room. "This room...it's weird. Every other room has been partially stripped. Why did they leave this one intact?"

"I don't know. Maybe it was Rachel's room and she was expecting to come back."

"Why would she leave her brush set behind?"

"I don't know, but…" A small smile played about Susan's lips. "I like this room. I like it a lot." She looked around, then back at Linda. "Dibs!"

Linda started. "What?"

"Dibs. You know, if we decide to not bunk together in the dining room."

"You really want to sleep in this mausoleum?"

Susan looked uncertain then, rubbing her arms.

The wind whistled around the eaves and Linda, watching Susan, caught a glimpse of movement just in the corner of her eye, a skirted figure hastening out of sight. When she turned, of course there was nothing but the wall and the vanity mirror reflecting her and Susan.

Don't even start, Linda, she chided herself.

The wind growled like a living being. For a moment, she could have sworn that the gloom had intensified. The storm was moving in fast, blocking what little light came through the shuttered windows. Soon it would be night and the darkness would be complete, without even the moon or stars to break it. It would be just the four of them; Michael with his hurt arm, pregnant Susan, Johnny, always one bad dream away from a melt-down, and herself.

Merry Christmas, Linda…

She was relieved when Susan broke the silence, "It's not creepy – it's the only room with furniture in the house. Anyway," she added, with a mischievous smile, "a woman in my condition shouldn't be sleeping on the floor."

Linda could not very well argue with that and agreed, provisionally, if the room did not prove too cold.

"Let's get out of here," she said. "If this room is that well preserved, I can't wait to see the master bedroom."

As it turned out, the master bedroom, an enormous room that took up fully a quarter of the house, with a large bathroom attached, and sweeping views (they imagined, anyhow, as the windows were also shuttered) of the river and mountains, was as stripped as the other rooms.

Linda, for the life of her, could not make sense of any of it.

CHAPTER 11

Without axes or saws, it took a lot of effort for the men to gather enough burnable materials for the night. Michael, although he did not complain, was favoring his sore arm and working slower than Johnny would wish. As the storm built up, adding new snow flurries to the already bitter cold winds coming off the river, it became a race against time. The only way to transport the wood was in their arms. They repeatedly trudged through the rapidly filling path dug by Johnny to drop loads of wood by the porch doors until they had a decently sized pile.

Johnny's cheeks were raw from the wind and his hands ached with cold while he sweated inside his coat from the exertion. He had pushed himself harder than was necessary simply to keep ahead of the storm. Michael said that he was going at army-speed without consideration for the civilian, but while Johnny laughed, he did not slacken his pace. Darkness was creeping through the trees and into the edges of his mind.

They took a breather on the porch. Michael was trying to make up his mind as to whether they still needed more wood. Johnny waited for him, rubbing his hands together to keep them warm and watching the river through the gap in the trees. The shore was lined with ice that extended several feet, highlighting the angry steel-gray water that churned past. Cold as it was, the river had still not frozen.

It probably looked the same that night, Johnny thought.

He hadn't been able to shake the Reynolds story out of his mind. The image of the mad man rushing through the snow with the bloody razor to throw himself off the dock played over and over in his head...

"What does it take to freeze that river?" he asked aloud, cutting through Michael's ruminations about possible burn speeds. "It's like Antarctica out here!"

It took a moment or two for Michael to answer, as though he were thumbing through the well-worn files of his mind. "The water gets deep fast on this side of the river. It's over eight feet at the end of the dock. When Charles jumped, he just plunged right in. Jacob didn't have a chance."

When Johnny looked at him, he explained: "Jacob North, my boss. He was the ward of Charles' grandfather and grew up with Charles. He was already outside when Charles ran out and he tried to stop him. They grappled on the dock but Charles was bigger and more determined. Jacob went in after him."

"Heroic."

"Very. He lost his coat in the river and caught pneumonia as a result. He almost died – took him weeks to recover." Michael looked down at the pile of wood and then up at the gathering storm. "I don't really relish the thought of coming out here in the middle of the night to replenish the fire, do you?"

Johnny shook his head. "No. Let's bring this inside. You can probably turn off that flashlight – I asked Linda to set up enough candles to light the main rooms."

"Oh, good! You know, between the fire, the candles, the appetizers, and the wine Linda brought, we have the makings of a fine night."

"Easy for you to say," Johnny said, following him into the darkened ballroom. "You were smart enough to bring your girl with you. All I have is my sister."

"That was poor planning," Michael laughed as he shouldered his way into the entryway. He stopped without warning and Johnny nearly ran into him.

"What gives?" Johnny asked, struggling to maintain hold of his load.

"No light," Michael grumbled and switched on his flashlight, which he was holding under his grip on the wood. He whistled. "Looks like the girls started the party without us."

He stepped aside and Johnny saw what he meant.

Both the dining room and the entryway were in nearly total darkness, though the faint scent of candle smoke indicated that some had been recently lit. As Michael's flashlight played about the room, they saw what appeared to be the aftermath of a paper-blizzard. Sheets, empty files, and tiny scraps of notepaper were scattered all over the floor, on the staircase, the banisters, and a few even hung from the cobweb-laced chandelier above them. A small table had been overturned, and a photo album lay open on its back, photos scattered about like blood spatters.

Michael's armload of wood hit the floor with a resounding crash.

"Susan?" He turned his light on the staircase, then towards the dining room. His voice went higher and louder: "Su*san*!"

Johnny was about to follow when he heard something on the floor above. He dropped his armload and his hand went to his hip, forgetting again that his firearm was at home, locked in his sister's safe. Johnny grasped a short, thick piece of wood instead and rose just as Linda's voice called to them, "Michael? Are you all right?"

Michael leapt for the stairs and climbed them two at a time, meeting the women on the landing. Johnny was a few steps behind him. Susan and Linda looked more concerned than frightened.

"Are you both all right?" Michael gasped.

"Of course," Susan said. "Why shouldn't we be?"

"We thought there'd been an intruder," Johnny said.

Linda frowned. "Why would you think that?"

Michael turned his flashlight to the entryway. Their collective gasp told Johnny the answer before Michael even asked the question, "Did you hear anything?"

"Nothing," Linda whispered.

"Where did all this paper come from?" Johnny asked.

Susan said, "It's a file Linda found in the living room. What happened? Could it have been the wind?"

Michael's flashlight lit up the overturned table – it was heavy oak with a marble top.

"Pretty strong wind," Michael said.

"Impossible," Johnny said.

"Maybe it was the ghost," Linda suggested, but it was a poor attempt at humor.

"Maybe we aren't alone," Michael said.

Part Two:
ATTRITION

CHAPTER 12

The decision to search the house from top to bottom was made without discussion. Michael and Susan went through the basement and the lower floors while Johnny and Linda took the attic and the second floor. Johnny did a double-take in Rachel's old room.

"This is just creepy," he said as they went back into the hallway.

"I know." Linda replied, feeling comforted by his reaction. "It's almost enough to make you believe in…"

She stopped short and jerked her head to look down the hallway. Johnny whipped around and pointed the flashlight. There was nothing to see but the glint of door knobs and the white of exposed wall under peeling paper.

"What is it?" he asked.

Linda shook her head. "Nothing," she said, glad that Johnny could not hear her pounding heart in the silence of that awful hallway. She was not about to admit that she had spotted movement where there could be none. "Just getting jumpy I guess. Where do you suppose the entrance to the attic is?"

They found a set of stairs in one of the end rooms. The attic was a vaulted, drafty chamber running the length of the house. It was unfinished, with boards nailed down for flooring and boxes piled up on either side with a middle lane kept clear for access. Low-hanging wires and light bulbs forced them to duck as they walked past.

Johnny checked around each pile with his flashlight. Linda stayed close to him, holding his wooden club. She listened keenly for the sound of another person; breathing, shifting, or movement. It was a fruitless effort. The wind was louder here than in the rest of the house and, if there had been noises, the wind would have masked them.

Johnny reached the far end of the attic and straightened up.

"Doesn't look like anyone's been here in decades," he said.

"Good," Linda replied.

He played his beam around the piles, stopping when he came to an artificial tree. "I guess this is where they kept the decorations."

"Great! If we are stuck here over Christmas, at least we can decorate."

"If the servants didn't sleep here," he said, "where did they sleep?"

She shrugged. "In the basement, maybe?"

"No. Michael and I were already down there. It's just a workspace."

"Then they must have stayed off the property," she said, and held her hand out. "Give me the flashlight, will you?"

He handed it over with some reluctance. She gave him the club, stepped over to the boxes, and opened one with her free hand. It gave easily, emitting a cloud of dust that set off a fit of sneezing. When her lungs cleared and she could see through her watery eyes, she peered into the box. Silver glittered in the beam of the flashlight.

"Take a look at this, Johnny! It's so *elegant*."

The box was packed tightly with tinsel, garland, and battered tins of gilt and green. The second box was more of the same and the third she opened was filled with wooden candy canes and stern nutcrackers in painted finery. Mingled with the dust was the scent of cinnamon and cloves, as though the memories of past Christmas celebrations had been packed along with the décor.

"This is just what we need," Linda said with satisfaction. When he looked at her in astonishment, she shoved a box at him. "Come on, sour puss. What we could use is a little Christmas atmosphere, don't you think?"

She would not hear any arguments and Johnny did not press too hard. With minimal grunting he hauled two of the boxes with the club balanced precariously on top while Linda led the way with the third box and the flashlight.

They found Michael and Susan in the entryway. Michael was playing his light around the area as though expecting the answer to seep out of cracks in the walls while Susan calmly collected the scattered papers.

"Look what we found!" Linda announced triumphantly. She lowered her box to the floor and pulled out a length of glittering garland. "We can have a proper Christmas now!"

Michael and Susan stared as Johnny dropped his load beside Linda's box.

"There was nothing but decorations in the attic," he said. "Did you find anything?"

"Nothing and no one," Michael affirmed. "We checked every closet, crawlspace, nook, and cranny. Nothing."

"So what happened here?"

Linda followed his gaze up to the chandelier. A few pages still wafted in the draft among the grime-covered crystals. The sight sent a shiver down her spine.

Michael shrugged. "Maybe Linda was right. It was the wind."

"Oh, come *on!*" Johnny snapped. It was like the crack of a whip.

Michael shot back, "Well, do *you* have a better explanation, smart guy?"

It was over as quickly as it started. The loss of his own temper surprised Michael. He looked at the floor and drew in a deep breath.

Linda and Susan exchanged nervous glances.

The wind and shadows, Linda thought. *They're getting to all of us.*

"Are you guys all right?" she asked.

Susan stepped in between the two men, her expression stern.

"We're all just a little tense," she said. "It's been a tough day."

There was rebuke in her tone, but Johnny seemed to think it was justified. He drew himself up and nodded an apology to Michael, who was rubbing his arm. He smiled back.

"Yeah," he said. "This place is spooky, is all."

For some reason, Linda wished he had not said that. Saying it out loud only seemed to aggravate the problem.

The explanation did not seem to bother Susan. She nodded briskly. "Well, we've proven that there's no one here, so the only thing left to explain this mess is the wind. Instead of getting in each other's faces, let's get this place secure and comfortable for the night. Bring in the wood, start the fire, and if you feel so inclined, lock or bar the doors. Linda and I will clean this up and then we'll eat. Okay?"

Her speech worked. Michael began to relax the minute Susan mentioned making the place secure. Johnny merely looked resigned, expecting the worst.

Probably wishing he had his bottle with him, Linda thought. *We've got no time for that here, Johnny.*

"All right," Johnny said, as though hearing her silent plea. "Let's start hauling wood, Mikey."

They left and Linda joined Susan in collecting papers. She felt guilty. Once again the younger, pregnant woman had to be the voice of reason while she herself stood aside and watched.

Someday, I'll be able to stand up and take control...

Susan cut into her thoughts, "The good news is, we found a butler's pantry between the ballroom and the kitchen. There are still dishes inside. We'll be able to eat like civilized human beings tonight."

"Well, that's something anyway," Linda said. But it was hard to work up anything like enthusiasm.

Above her head, the chandelier swayed gently in the breeze.

CHAPTER 13

After some discussion, the living room was selected as the central location, thanks to its relatively clean looking fireplace. The flue opened to release some dead leaves, twigs, and, even more promising, snow.

"That means it isn't closed off," Michael said.

"I wouldn't count on it being swept, though," Johnny said darkly. "We'll have to keep a close eye."

Michael built the fire while Johnny helped the others bring their things in from the dining room. They raided the butler's pantry and found dishes, utensils, towels, more candles, matches, and even a few lanterns.

"Excellent," Susan said. "We'll be going through a lot of these tonight, I think."

The firewood being wet with snow, it took Michael awhile to get the fire started and there was a universal sigh of relief once it was blazing comfortably. The crackle and snap of burning wood, the welcomed warmth and light, was like an old friend come to visit. Michael and Johnny had already shed their coats. Now Linda felt warm enough to do the same. Susan, however, kept hers on.

It was 6:30 before everything was set up and Michael declared it too early for dinner.

"Why don't we start decorating?" he asked. When Susan looked blank-eyed at him, he explained, "Linda's right. Just because we're snowed in for the night doesn't mean we can't celebrate the holiday."

It was a transparent attempt to lighten the mood, but Linda did not care. She hopped up and said with more eagerness than she really felt, "Oh, yes, let's!"

Johnny and Susan were noticeably reluctant. They stepped forward to help when Michael, in a moment of exaggerated enthusiasm, dumped the box of garland and tinsel in the middle of the floor. Linda threw herself on the ground next to the pile and began to pull pieces out.

"Don't dump the other box," she warned. "I think the glass stuff is in there."

"It won't be a proper Christmas without a tree," Susan observed.

"There's a tree in the attic," Linda said, looking significantly at Johnny. "It's fake, but still..."

Johnny sighed in mock annoyance. "Fine, I'll get it."

"I'll help!" Michael said.

When the two men had left, Susan said to Linda, "If we're going to decorate, we're going to do it properly – with taste and balance."

"Of course!" Linda stood up with an armful of garland. "Where do you suggest we start?"

By the time the men returned, Linda had resigned all creative decisions to Susan. The blonde threw herself into decorating with a passion no one expected, directing the placement of garland, candy canes, and angels, ordering Michael to move the tree to the other side of the room, scolding Johnny

TALE HALF TOLD

laughingly when he hung the snowflakes askew. She had Linda running all about the room, fetching this and moving that. She insisted that the mantelpiece be decorated just so and did it herself.

"Go into the pantry and see if you can find silver candlesticks," she instructed Linda.

Linda was too relieved to see Susan looking alert and interested to mind being bossed about. She found two silver candlesticks in the pantry, elegantly wrought and surprisingly unmarred by tarnish, and bore them triumphantly back into the living room. She stopped just inside the door to stare.

"Oh my goodness!" she exclaimed. "This room has been transformed!"

And so it had. The light from the candles and the fire refracted off the silver decorations, making the room both brighter and cozier than when they had first seen it. The mixing shadows hid the worst of the room's neglect. The two men, setting up a chess board now that the tree was finished, brought life and sound to the room.

If I saw this in any other house, Linda thought, happily, *I'd say it looked like a picture postcard.*

Susan, fussing about the mantelpiece, noticed her standing in the doorway. "Oh, good, you found them! Bring them here."

She placed them at the opposite ends of the mantelpiece while Linda looked around the room with admiration.

"You really do have a terrific eye, Susan," she said.

"You've got that right," Michael volunteered. "She turned our house into a showpiece."

"Well, that settles it, then," Linda said as Susan stepped back for a critical look at the mantelpiece. "I'm hiring you to do over my apartment."

66

Susan pursed her lips, less than satisfied. "It would look better if we had a little Christmas tree in the middle," she said, tilting her head as she spoke, "with a dove on top."

"A dove? Not a star?"

"A dove would be best, I think." She looked around the room and folded her arms. "Well. That's it, then. We're ready for the big man in red."

"That's not until tomorrow night," Johnny said. "Hopefully we won't be here *that* long."

"Amen," Michael said. He was rubbing his injured arm again.

Now that the decorating was through, Linda felt the chill, raw edge of nervousness creeping up on her again. She busied herself to keep from growing uneasy, repacking the unused decorations in the cardboard boxes and wiping down the glasses and dishes that they planned to use at dinner. The room was quiet. The snap and steady hum of the fire contrasted pleasantly with the roar of the wind outside. Michael and Johnny played quietly, with occasional jocular threats of prowess. Linda wished they had a radio. Some cheery carols would have taken the edge off the isolation and covered the pregnant silence of the house.

No use wishing for what you can't have.

Susan stood by the fireplace, wrapped in thought, idly rubbing her stomach. She looked pale, even in the warm glow. Her reverie was unlike her usual self – Susan was not really the introspective type. In any social situation, she was the one taking charge, making noise.

She's nervous, Linda thought. *Probably still worried about the baby.*

Linda could not blame her. Both of them had too much hospital experience to bluff their way into thinking everything was alright. But there was nothing to be gained by worrying. Until symptoms manifested or they had the means to examine her properly, there was nothing they could do. Worrying only added to the already palpable tension the situation engendered.

Suddenly, as though aware she was being thought of, Susan turned from the fire and announced, "I'm going to take a nap. I'm wiped out."

Something in her voice, a sterile, flat sound, made Linda jump up and go over to her. She placed her hand on Susan's arm. The younger woman looked at her, her eyes dark, indecipherable wells.

"Are you okay, honey?" Michael asked.

Susan nodded, breaking eye contact with Linda. "Oh, fine, just exhausted. It's been a long day."

"Want me to make up the couch for you?" Linda asked.

"Oh no, I'll use Rachel's room." When she saw Michael staring at her, she explained, "It'll be quiet and comfortable, and it's right over this room. The chimney must run through it. I'll be perfectly warm in there."

Michael didn't like it, but, of course, Susan had her way. Linda grabbed an armful of blankets and a spare box of matches and gripped Susan's arm firmly as they made their way up the sweeping staircase.

"You don't need to come," Susan said. "I'm fine."

Linda didn't reply to that.

The room seemed to have grown even darker and gloomier since they'd last seen it. Linda found herself thinking if one waited long enough in that darkness, it would seep inside them through pores and orifices, until one blended with the shadows and lost all sense of self.

Oh, for crying out loud, Linda! Pull yourself together!

She shook herself out of it. She had no time for romantic illusions about the dark. She was a nurse with a patient who needed rest.

Linda went to work checking the mattress. There wasn't enough light for her to see properly and anyway, as Susan said, no insect could have survived the cold. Susan waited patiently for Linda to spread out the blankets and play with the candle, making sure it was in a draft-free position. Finally, tired of the fussing, she ordered Linda out.

"I'll be fine," she insisted. She lay on the bed, curled in a fetal position, hair spread like a starburst around her. "I'm really very tired, Linda. Please let me sleep."

"Are you sure you're all right?" Linda lowered her voice even though she knew they were alone. "Are you... feeling anything?"

"I'm just so tired. Please shut the door." Susan sounded exhausted and very, very young.

There being no real reason to stay in the room, Linda did as she was asked.

She paused outside in the hallway. The darkness hovered thickly here too, anxious to overwhelm the tenuous light of her one candle. She listened at Susan's door, hearing nothing but the faint murmur of the men's voices downstairs. A draft brushed her shoulders, reminding her that she had left her coat downstairs.

She's all right, Linda chided herself. *Anyway, there's nothing you can do about it now. Sleep's the best thing for her.*

She had not gone more than a half dozen steps down the hallway when her candle flickered violently, nearly going out. As she threw up a hand to protect the flame, something, *someone,* bumped against her hip, knocking her against the wall. She squeaked as she struck the plaster, managing not to scream. A flurry of footsteps pattered past her, rushing up to the end of the hall, vanishing there.

Then there was silence.

Linda was frozen against the wall, her thoughts racing: *They're at the end of the hall. They're standing there, watching me.*

Yet she had seen nothing. When her trembling hands raised the candle, the light was barely able to reach the back wall. There was nothing there but undisturbed cobwebbing.

She pressed a hand to her beating heart.

It was nothing. You imagined it. You're going to give yourself a heart attack if you don't stop this.

She went back to listen at Susan's door, too embarrassed to open it and admit her fright. All was quiet inside. She hurried to the staircase and stopped at the top for one more look before descending.

She saw nothing and told herself the faint giggle that she heard was one of the men below, laughing at a clever move.

CHAPTER 14

When Linda returned, she was pale and nervous and gratefully accepted the wine Johnny offered.

"Thanks. This house is starting to get to me."

She did not elaborate and neither of the men asked. They played chess while Linda settled down by the fireplace with her glass and the pile of pages.

Time crept by slowly. A comfortable quiet reigned. The storm outside provided white noise in the background. The fire snapped and popped.

As the game drew to a conclusion, Michael began to grow restless. The wine was good, but served to remind him of how hungry he was and he worried about Susan. When Johnny left to use the gents, Michael checked his watch. Only an hour had gone by since Susan went upstairs, yet he felt as though it had been much longer.

Susan must have been exhausted, he thought. *It isn't like her to nap.*

He got up to stretch his legs. Linda was still hard at work by the fireplace. Her wine glass sat close at hand, half full and forgotten. She had pulled her reddish-brown hair up into a bun and donned her heavy-framed glasses. The glasses were a sign Michael had come to recognize. Linda was too vain to wear them regularly, only putting them on when she was concentrating hard. She frowned as she leaned toward the light of the dampening fire, studying the newspaper clippings.

"Finding anything interesting?" he asked, as he squatted down to rebuild the fire.

She took off her glasses and tapped the page she was holding. "Susan and I found this in the study," she said. "It looks like Rachel kept everything to do with the Othello killings. Look…"

She began to spread the material out on the floor. Michael craned his neck to watch as she continued: "There are newspaper clippings, magazine articles, photos, sheets of handwritten notes… Most of it is from the time of the killing. It's creepy. I mean, the murder happened in her own house, in her own family. She collected memorabilia like she was one of those obsessive types who get a kick out of serial killer stories. And look at this." She held up a magazine article with a photo. "I've figured out whose room it is that Rachel kept fully furnished upstairs."

The picture showed an elegant bedroom with a tall, well-dressed elderly Rachel Reynolds standing proudly in the middle. The headline read, *'Murder Room Reveals New Clues, claims relative.'*

"It's Helene's room," Michael said.

Linda nodded and pointed to the side table in the picture. "See that music box? It's still up there. Isn't that weird?"

Michael had to agree. "They say that Rachel is an eccentric."

"I think they are understating the case."

He chuckled and picked up another newspaper clipping, this one dated January 3rd, 1947. There was a picture of a young man in a hospital bed, hooked up to a variety of IVs and machines and looking at the camera with an impassive expression. A woman sat at his bedside glaring at the camera, her hand grasping his as though to protect him from harm. The headline read, '*Heroic Sacrifice: Exclusive Interview with Jacob North.*'

"Funny to see the boss looking so young," Michael said.

She leaned over to look at it. "So that's what he looks like. Somehow I pictured someone more intimidating."

"Don't sell him short. He's recovering from pneumonia in this picture: anyone is bound to look a little withered." He handed the photo back, commenting, "That's his wife next to him. She was Irene Simmons then."

"The one who died here?"

Michael nodded and rubbed his throbbing arm. "She was the daughter of the housekeeper. She and Jacob practically grew up together. The family credits her with saving him from pneumonia, but they didn't like her much. When she married Jacob, Rachel Reynolds accused her of using him to climb the social ladder."

"What do you think?"

He shrugged. "Maybe she did. I don't know. Frankly, I don't think Jacob North is a man easily used by anyone. People who know them say they were well matched. She was just as ambitious."

She nodded. "What kind of man is Jacob North?"

It was a good question. Michael did not know Jacob very well personally. The familial connection was distant and the Norths were not the sort to host reunions. He did have occasion to meet Jacob at various company events, though, and one thing was certain - the man was striking.

"He's not very tall, but he carries himself like he is," Michael said. "He was orphaned young and wasn't able to fight in the war because he was near-sighted. Instead, he threw himself into running the business while Charles was making himself a war hero. But Jacob wasn't the heir, Charles was, and when Charles came home, Jacob was expected to hand everything back over to him. Then Charles died and the family fell apart, so Jacob had to step up again. In the end, he saved the business and the family reputation, and everything went to him." He looked at the photo again, shaking his head. "A real rags-to-riches story. Quite a man."

"Sounds like you admire him," Linda said.

"I guess I do. He's an example of how perseverance can triumph over breeding, but he's not an easy man to like. He's studiously polite, but he doesn't have many friends. Even Rachel flat-out refused to let him or his wife into this house again."

"Oh? Why not?"

He shrugged. "Most people think it's because she hasn't forgiven him for not saving Charles. I don't think he's ever been able to get over the fact that he wasn't a Reynolds, or a war hero like Charles."

"Echoes," Linda murmured. When he looked at her, she explained, "The past. We say it's dead, don't we? But it's not, not really. It echoes or, I guess, causes ripples that affect the present and the future. Charles fights in a war and dies at home. His death gives both great guilt and great power to a man whose every business decision affects you, to some degree anyway. It's like how Johnny is now - wrestling with what happened overseas. He's trapped by it, unable to recover or move on." She sighed. "Are we ever truly free of the past?"

The question surprised Michael.

"I supposed we are as trapped by it as we want to be," he said after a moment. "You're right. We are shaped by it to a point. The confines of this room, built by others long before the Reynolds, dictate how much furniture can be put in here. The Reynolds, however, are only really confined if they never look beyond this room's existing four walls. I suppose our lives are the same."

There was a long silence. Then Linda said, "Are you sure it was accounting you studied, Mikey? Or is philosophy a byproduct of financial wisdom?"

He laughed. "I think it's all those episodes of the Twilight Zone I used to watch."

"Remind me to start watching them, too," she quipped, rummaging through more pages. "Wait – did you just say Irene was forbidden from entering this house?"

Michael nodded. "Yes. Rachel resented a Simmons marrying into the Reynolds family business, even if only to an adopted family member. Anyway, about ten years ago, Rachel was getting ready to move to her winter place in Florida. Irene came with one of the cousins to help her pack, despite Rachel's objections. I think she was trying to mend the wound. That's when she had the accident; fell down the flight of stairs in the middle of the night and broke her neck."

It was a part of the story that never quite made sense to Michael. Irene Simmons North was a spry, active woman in good health and not disposed to drinking or drug use. She'd gone to bed in the old house, after helping a protesting old Rachel box up her valuables. Later that night, Rachel and the others heard a scream. They found Irene at the bottom of the stairs, wide-eyed and contorted. *"Looked as though the Devil himself had been chasing her,"* was the exact quote on the report. Rachel's live-in paid companion claimed that she heard Irene running in the hall just before the scream, but as she was an excitable personality prone to exaggeration, her testimony was discredited as unprovable. Jacob North, crushed by his wife's death, decided against investigating further, a move that surprised everyone, and the matter of Irene's death remained shrouded in doubt.

I suppose people do just fall, Michael thought. But it didn't sound any better this time than it had before.

Linda broke into his thoughts: "Tragic. Jacob must have been devastated."

He drew in a breath and nodded. "Yes… And it really shook Rachel. She had a nervous breakdown shortly after. Probably why she left her research locked up in a drawer, rather than take it with her."

"Poor thing. So much tragedy in her house." Linda held up an article. "On another note, why didn't Susan tell me that Charles returned maimed from the war? According to this, he lost his right hand and was also undergoing psychiatric treatment when he killed his wife." She handed him the clipping. "Was she afraid to tell me because of Johnny?"

Michael shrugged and studied the article. It was an interview with Rachel Reynolds, dated 1958.

Odd, he thought. *I've never seen this before. I thought I read everything to do with this house…*

"It's not like I ever stop worrying about Johnny," Linda was saying. "But knowing this makes it easier to understand why a war hero with a brilliant future ahead of him suddenly goes mental and ends it all."

"You know how it was in those days," Michael murmured. "People were embarrassed to mention psychiatric problems, especially a high profiler like Charles Reynolds. As for his treatment, Charles was…" He broke off suddenly when Johnny came striding back into the room.

Johnny grinned and squatted down next to them.

"What's all this?" he asked.

"Rachel Reynolds' secret files on the Othello killing," Linda said. "We're trying to figure out why she compiled such a gruesome collection."

"Maybe she liked spooky, insane murders."

"Pretty tame novel collection, if that was the case."

Michael broke in impatiently, "Where did you find this interview, Linda? I've never seen this before."

"It was there, among the rest." Linda waved her hand over the pile. "I don't know which file it was in; everything got mixed up in the hall. Is the interview any good? I haven't read it yet."

"If you had read the last paragraph, it would have answered your question about Rachel's collection," Michael said, and read aloud:

As our interview comes to a close, she rises like a queen from her seat and escorts me to the door, still talking about her plans and hopes. She speaks calmly, thoughtfully, deliberately. In the face of all the evidence, Ms. Reynolds is determined to prove her theory is correct.

"There is no way Charles would have killed his wife," she says as we say our goodbyes. "Someday, before I die, I intend to prove it."

"That does explain the collection," Linda said. "But how can she possibly think that she could prove Charles' innocence? There were all those witnesses! Look, there's a copy of the testimony here…"

She dug through the pile and pulled out a yellowed stack of carefully type-written paper, stapled together with the heading of the district court on it. "There are a dozen depositions from guests, all saying the same thing: Charles Reynolds came into the ballroom with the razor in his hand, blood on his shirt, and a crazed look in his eye. Half of them watched from the patio when he plunged into the river with Jacob."

"But did anyone see him actually kill Helene?" Johnny spoke absently, shifting through the various pages that were spread out on the floor around him.

"No," Michael said. "No one saw that."

Linda followed up with, "But there's only one exit and entrance into Helene's room and it was under observation the whole time. A married couple, the Abernathys, were having an argument on the landing. They saw Charles go into the room shortly before midnight, and stumble out again about fifteen minutes later, covered in blood. No one else went in or out."

"We know that Helene was killed in that half-hour period," Michael chimed in. "She'd gone up early with a migraine. Irene was the nurse attending both Helene and Charles and she went up with a maid at 11:15 to give her aspirin. Both testified that Helene was alive when they left and there's no reason to suspect that either would lie. Neither gained anything from the affair."

"Except that Irene married the eventual heir," Johnny pointed out.

"They were already engaged before the murder," Michael said. "It wasn't announced because this party was supposed to be a belated 'Welcome Home' party for Charles. It was a big deal. Helene and Rachel spent a good deal of money on it. There was even a fight over the amount of money Helene spent having a special music box made for Charles."

When the two siblings looked at him, Michael grinned.

"My mother may have only been a distant cousin," he said, "but she likes to hobnob and pick up gossip. When she learned I was interested in the Reynolds' matter, she invited me to Sunday lunch and told me everything she knew. For instance, the family wasn't thrilled about Helene. Charles met her in France where she was working as a nurse, and married her there, thus dashing all hopes that he might marry into the New

York set. Lionel Reynolds, his grandfather, even hired detectives to look into her background, trying to discover if there was anything annullable in her past. They didn't find anything. Eventually the Reynolds had to accept the fact that they had a French girl for their pride and joy, not a Philadelphian or New York heiress. It was a great disappointment."

"But not grounds for a murder that would send Charles over the edge," Johnny mused.

"Even if there was opportunity," Michael conceded, "which there wasn't."

Linda sighed. "Honestly, the more I read about Charles, the more I like him and the less I want to believe he killed his wife."

"Me, too," Michael said. "But it does fit the facts. Killing someone with a razor is hardly the method of cold-blooded killer who hopes to get away with it. It's too messy. It's what you use in a fit of rage. At least, that's what the police said." He paused, then went on. "And then there is Charles' doctor's testimony. According to him, Charles was having a... hard time adjusting to civilian life. His time on the battlefield, incarceration in a German POW camp, the accident that cost him his hand, and then later, when he aided in processing the rescued from the concentration camps- all of it left him shattered."

Linda glanced at Johnny. He was flipping, unconcerned, through a magazine. "He was on medications, wasn't he?" he asked.

"Charles was on medication for a variety of symptoms, but the lawyers pointed out three specifics." Michael counted them off on his fingers. "His growing paranoia, his occasional temper flare-ups, and his blackouts. Apparently, he didn't even start seeing a psychologist until after three episodes where he'd blacked out and woken unaware of what had happened to him in the preceding hours.

"According to the help, Charles and Helene had an argument shortly before the party, contributing, they thought, to her migraine. The argument had been about some rumors regarding Helene and one of the electricians who'd been helping to re-wire the house. Plus, when the autopsy was done, Charles was shown to have ingested almost twice the amount of medication than was prescribed. Both Charles' psychiatrist and his physician thought it very likely that a combination of the paranoia and the overdose created the elements needed for murder."

"Yikes," Johnny muttered.

Linda sighed in frustration. "Honestly, with what I've read so far, I'm at a loss to explain Rachel's stubborn insistence that Charles was innocent."

Michael shrugged. "She grew to like Helene and adored Charles. According to the family, she was so devastated by the loss she simply couldn't accept it. Everyone was relieved when she finally left this place and went to Florida for good." He shivered as he looked around. "It's a shame that a beautiful place like this should be kept only as a monument to the dead."

"A museum, you mean," Linda said. "She kept Helene's room almost exactly the same for twenty-five years - creepy."

"That's not the creepiest thing that's happened in this house," Johnny said suddenly.

They both turned to him. He was holding up a magazine with both hands, his gaze shifting from the page to the mantelpiece.

"What do you mean?" Linda asked.

She sounds, Michael thought, *like she really doesn't want to know.*

Johnny raised his hand to his head, as though to brush back a lock of hair from his face. He froze when he found nothing there. Then he looked at them.

"How much of this material has Susan seen?" he asked sharply.

"She just glanced at it, why?" Linda said.

Johnny shook his head. "No, I mean you, Michael. When you were doing your research on this place for the company, did you bring stuff home with you? Did she see any photos?"

Michael frowned. "No. She wasn't interested at all. I didn't bring home anything anyway – it was kind of spooky and I didn't want to… why are you asking?"

Johnny looked at him warily. "She seemed awfully insistent on how this place ought to be decorated. Almost as if she had an image in mind. Almost as if she'd seen this."

He turned the page around for them to see. There, in glossy black and white, was a picture of two women – a willowy young blonde and a curvy brunette several years her senior. They were dressed in casual wear from the forties and the blonde woman was laughing, her hands on the mantelpiece. She was adjusting a small Christmas tree. The caption read, '*Hours before her gruesome death, Helene Fournier Reynolds decorates with her aunt by marriage, Rachel.*'

Michael looked at the mantelpiece. With the exception of the missing Christmas tree, it looked exactly as it did in the photo – right down to the silver candlesticks on either end.

"Oh my God," Linda whispered. "That tree… in the picture. There's a dove on it."

The wind crashed about the eaves.

CHAPTER 15

Susan was dreaming. She had gone to sleep almost as soon as Linda had left, falling into one of those deep, dreamless voids where sleep is almost like a drug. Then images began to invade her peace.

She was in the car again, bracing herself against the back of the seat, watching as the tree rushed up to meet them. Linda was shouting, but Susan could not speak. The pain in her abdomen was too severe. She tried to scream, but sound would not come.

The dream ended on impact, only to start over. Again and again she lived through that accident, feeling the terror, the pain, the shards of glass as they showered over her. The details were vivid, more real than reality; from the tension in her legs, bracing for impact, to the sound of metal hitting wood, and the taste of blood in her mouth.

Then the details started to change.

One time it was not Michael who was driving the car, but a strange man. He was trying to tell her something. The look in his eyes was searing, but the crash interrupted them. In the next, it was Michael again and he was saying, "This isn't what is happening, Susie. This isn't what is happening," while she screamed, "But it is!" In another dream, she was holding two children in her arms when they crashed. She was still clutching them when Johnny pulled her out of the wreckage. They were crying out to her in French, their blood-spattered faces turning from cherubic to demonic as she watched.

The last was the worst. The car wrapped around the tree, trapping Susan in her seat with her legs pinned under the dashboard. Michael died on impact, his head resting on her shoulder, his blood ruining her coat. She screamed for Linda and Johnny, but they did not answer and she knew that she was alone. Snow began to pile up, burying the car, burying her. She tried, frantically, to free herself from the wreckage, crying for Michael to wake, for someone to help, but no one heard and the snow kept coming. Then, just as she was about to be buried alive, she caught a glimpse of movement on the driveway. As she twisted to look, she saw a cloaked figure watching, standing on the crest where they had just slid. The figure made no movement to help. The last thing Susan knew before the dream ended was that the figure had somehow caused the accident.

And then it was over and she was awake. She was in her room, alone. She could hear the sounds of the others from downstairs, laughing as they made merry. The room was dark and the music box was playing, '*I'll be home for Christmas... You can plan on me...*'

Susan heard a sound. The darkness shifted, coalescing into a shape, a figure. There was someone in the room, standing over her. A hand covered her mouth. She turned to look at him. The face was obscured, but she knew him. She knew him well enough to be surprised when he lifted the razor.

Susan screamed.

CHAPTER 16

Michael was half-way down the hall, on his way to wake Susan and still musing over Johnny's weird discovery, when he heard it. The fear-tortured scream was almost beyond recognition, but he knew it to be Susan's. He was in her room in an instant.

It was dark in Helene's room. Murkiness hung heavily over everything, threatening to overwhelm the sputtering candle that Linda had left on the bedside table. It was so frigid and clammy that Michael wondered why Linda let Susan sleep in here. It *felt* like a tomb, but oddly, smelled of cinnamon and cloves — and fear.

Susan was sitting bolt-up right on the bed, clutching an afghan to her chest protectively. Her face was elongated in a now-soundless scream. She stared at the far side of the room as the tinny sounds of a music box faded away.

"Susan?" Michael's voice sounded faint against the hammering of his heart.

She turned to him. Her eyes were huge, dark pools against her ashen face.

"Il est la!" she gasped. "Il est *la!*" She gestured toward the far side of the room.

Michael ran around the end of the bed. The darkness was thick here, resistant to the light of his flashlight. There was a noticeable drop in the already low temperature. He found only a desk, a stuffed chair, and a closet, smelling of mothballs and filled with old women's clothing. No one hid among them.

It was only then, when Michael was looking around for an impossible intruder, that he realized that Susan had spoken to him in French.

He looked at his wife. She was sitting rigidly, watching him with a twisted sort of sneer.

"Ou est votre manteau?" Michael's wife spoke, but not with Susan's voice.

"Is everything all right in here?"

Michael jumped and turned. Johnny stood silhouetted in the door, holding a candle in his hand and the club in the other. He flinched when the light of Michael's flashlight hit his face, but he did not move.

"I heard a scream," he said.

Michael drew a long shuddering breath and nodded. "Susan. She…"

He realized that she was no longer sitting up. She had fallen back onto the bed, her face peaceful and her beautiful hair spread out around her like a fan. One hand was resting on her stomach and the other was curled up near her face. She looked so still that for a moment, Michael was afraid. When she stirred gently, he almost fell backwards in relief.

"She thought she saw someone," he said. "She must have been dreaming."

Johnny looked at her, then at Michael. "You checked?"

Michael drew himself up, stung. "Of course I did."

The other man nodded, but his pose remained rigid.

"What's the matter?" Linda appeared at Johnny's side. "Is Susan all right?"

Susan emitted a low moan. Linda elbowed her way past Johnny. Michael helped Susan sit up, supporting her as she tried to shake the sleep out of her eyes. Linda made soothing noises, while Johnny prowled about the perimeter of the room, his sharp eyes scanning the shadows.

I already looked, Michael thought furiously as Susan nestled deeper into his embrace. *Do you think I wouldn't be concerned with my own wife's safety?*

Susan was coming to now. Linda said, "Did you have a nightmare, honey?"

The candle light made Linda appear older than she was but Susan only looked more beautiful, even with her hair mussed and her make-up smudged with sleep and tears.

"Did I?" Susan sounded surprised. "I don't know. What are you all doing here?" She looked up at Michael.

She spoke French. Susan doesn't speak French. He tightened his grip on her, drawing her close as though by holding her, he could shield her. *First my macabre curiosity nearly got everyone killed, now my wife is being tormented by nightmares. This is all my fault. We never should have come here...*

"We heard you scream, Susan," Linda explained. "Were you dreaming?"

"Well... I guess I must have been. I don't remember. Except..."

"Except?"

"Except..." She hesitated and looked at her hands. "It just seemed awfully real, is all. I thought – I dreamed that there was a man, standing over my bed, holding a...a razor. He put one hand on my mouth and with the other, he..." She lifted a hand, as though to imitate the movement of the razor, and then she froze, her eyes wide with realization. Her other hand went to her protectively to her throat. "He was going to…"

"Susan" Linda said gently. "It was just a dream."

Susan started at the sound. She dropped both hands into her lap, looked at Linda, and tried to smile. "Oh, yes, of course, you're right. I guess – I guess I've been thinking too much about that murder."

Michael caught the expression on Linda's face: she looked as though all life was draining out of her.

Johnny broke the sudden silence. "Better get her out of here," he said, without coming away from the far end of the room. "It's just getting colder."

Linda nodded, hopping down from the bed. "Yes, best thing for you is a hot drink, a warm fire, and some food."

"You're probably right," Susan said. "That'll teach me to go to bed without eating."

She laughed, but Michael knew his wife too well to believe that she had recovered. She was talking a little too loudly, agreeing a little too quickly. And, proving him correct, Susan swayed when she stood up, almost losing her balance. Michael caught her and put his hand around her waist.

"Let me lend you a strong man's arm, honey," he said.

He tried to keep his tone light. To his surprise, Susan leaned into him, shivering. He could feel her recovering strength as wakefulness returned in full and he thought again, *This is all my fault. We never should have come.*

Linda ran on ahead to start making the drinks. Michael and Susan were out the door before they realized that Johnny wasn't following. Michael stepped back inside. Johnny was still wandering around the far end of the room, frowning at the closet.

"Are you coming?" Michael asked.

"I'll be along." When Michael hesitated, Johnny waved him off impatiently. "I'll just be a minute. Go ahead!"

"Suit yourself. If you take too long, I can't promise there'll be any food left."

"I'll be along. Just want to satisfy my curiosity, that's all."

Michael couldn't imagine what he meant, but decided it didn't matter at the moment. Susan was his primary concern. As he walked his wife slowly down that long hallway, it occurred to him how much warmer it was there than it had been in Helene's room.

Then Susan spoke. "Michael," she said, softly, "that bedroom *is* Helene's room, isn't it?"

Michael decided not to ask her how she knew that.

CHAPTER 17

Being in a darkened, creepy room with other people was one thing. Being alone in the same room was quite another, Johnny decided. It was as though the darkness, the clamminess, and loneliness itself waited until the others had gone before crowding back in to try and overwhelm him. He could feel fear reaching for him with icy tentacles, sucking him back into the vortex of memory, guilt, and horror.

*I will **not** give in. I will **not** give in.*

Johnny had stayed behind initially to take a closer look at the room. He could not quite believe that they were alone in the house. Susan was not fanciful enough to invent a figure at the end of her bed and no mere draft overturned that table earlier. They were not alone. Johnny was convinced that he would find evidence of this somewhere in this room. But though he searched thoroughly, he found only suffocating darkness and resurging self-doubt.

There's nothing here but my overactive imagination. I should leave.

He should have, but he wouldn't, not yet. He had experienced panic attacks often enough to recognize the symptoms — shortness of breath, sweating, nausea, detachment from his surroundings. They always came upon him suddenly, but Johnny was getting quicker at identifying them. He wouldn't leave until it subsided.

He paced, back and forth, back and forth, fighting himself, fighting the darkness, fighting the memories, fighting the nightmare that was always poised to take over reality. But he would not leave the room. He would not seek the sanctuary of the noise and companionship downstairs. Not until he'd faced this down and beat it.

*I will **not** give in. Not now. Not ever.*

Cowards gave in, weaklings. He had known a few. Some never made it out of the jungles. Some never made it off the ship home. Some came home, kissed their wives, and quietly went insane in the supposed sanctuary of their homes. Others drank or did dope to keep the demons at bay. Alcohol was Johnny's drug of choice, not that drinking helped much. It was only temporary relief, until he fell asleep and the dreams began. Once he had naively thought that all he needed was to get out of the jungle, away from the fighting, and return state-side. He had thought that he would find peace once he was out of the army and out of the line of fire. He had been wrong. You could leave the jungle, but 'Nam came home with you, tucked in a hidden pocket of your mind, tenacious. Insidious. Relentless. Overwhelming.

I will not give in. I will not.

Pacing was not working, so he tried a different tactic. He sat on the foot of the bed and bent over with his elbows pressed against his knees. He breathed slowly.

In and out.

In and out.

I will beat this. I am stronger.

He did not know why his attack was so strong or why this house dredged up the old memories. There was nothing here, really, to remind him of Vietnam. It was a simply a northern house with a bad history not related to him in anyway.

Except for Charles Reynolds, of course…he had been in the military too, and had come home with the nightmares. Like Johnny, they had put him on pills and told him that he would be alright with a few therapy sessions. Only they had been wrong. Charles fought the same battle twenty-five years ago and lost.

I will *not lose. I'll beat this. I will not give in.*

Why not give in?

It was the same old question, the one he had faced a dozen times before. Why not give in? Why not accept the new reality, this broken version of himself, the gaping wound that would never heal. Men did not revert back to boys. Pandora's box could never be closed. Too many soldiers who went into the jungles never came home again.

You can't win. You've already lost.

He buried his face in his hands, tremors running the length of his body. Memories surged through him; the jungle, the snap of gunfire, the panic in his chest, knowing death was always just out of sight, the bodies lined up in the sun, awaiting burial, the smells, the burns, and the fear. Fear was the one companion who never left your side, no matter how many bullets whipped past or how far you were from the frontlines. For months he braved the enemies of freedom, democracy, and the American way of life in places he had never heard of until a week before he deployed.

Then he came home.

He had not expected a parade or medals – the war was not over yet, after all – but he had expected at least a happy reception for the straggling remains of his platoon when their plane landed at the airport. What they got was a crowd of protesters with signs and slogans: "Get out now", "To What End?", and "Self-Determination for Vietnam." A few of the signs said, "Save our Soldiers," but they weren't what Johnny remembered. He could still recall men and women his own age screaming at him, calling him a murderer. One woman spat on him as he passed.

"Imperialist puppet!" she screamed.

There was nothing to be done. He walked on, ignoring her. He could still see the blank expressions on his companions' faces, except, of course, for the Colonel. He was beet-red and shaking with fury. But like the rest, he was determinedly silent. And Johnny began to wonder if the woman had not been right.

It was all for nothing. All for nothing. You bloodied your hands to advance what? The political machinations of fat cats in Washington?

Johnny was tired of this, tired of fighting and the moral struggle, tired of seeing the war on the news, in the papers, on television. He was so deadly tired of forever wanting to forget and never quite managing it. He gave in to the memories. Immersing himself again in the muck, in the blood, in the jungle, he was so deep in the past he didn't hear the door slam open against the wall. He felt the warmth, the humidity, the bite of the M1 Garand jumping in his hand, the smell of burning brush and flesh. Memories shifted and melded into each other. Saigon blended into Japan and into places he barely remembered. He was in the jungle, and then he was in the camp. He tasted dry air, felt the perpetual cold seep into his bones, writhed in pain from the wound that kept him bed-bound for weeks. The explosion had knocked him off his feet and left him unconscious and wounded on the hillside for the enemy to pick up. Trapped, caught, useless, in ever-present pain. The memories swirled again: the guerillas, the marching, the ovens, the emaciated bodies, the pathetic, frightened looks of ones behind the barbed wire.

"How could we know that you were cowboys, riding to the rescue?" one had said.

"They will never trust again, after what they've been through," Joe told him, "and who can blame them, Chuck?"

His hand ached unbearably. The memories surged like a tidal wave, overwhelming him, drowning him, until he could hear nothing but the sound of his own thoughts.

Stop it, stop it, stop it…!

When Johnny began to run, it was with one thought in mind – to drown the thoughts in his head before he was lost in them forever.

CHAPTER 18

Susan was ill. Michael was sure of it. She was ghostly white and trembled even as she tried to reassure him that she was all right. He didn't believe her. All of Linda's protests that she was physically fine only convinced him that the two women were lying to him.

Linda sent Michael out to fill a pitcher with snow while she settled Susan down with an afghan and a mug. Michael did as she instructed. It was bitterly cold outside and he filled the pitcher hastily. Quick as he was, his ears were cold and sore before he pulled his head back into the relative warmth of the house.

"This place is a regular ice-box," he grumbled to himself. "Must have cost a fortune to heat back in the day."

Michael was crossing the entryway with his hands full when Johnny burst out from the hallway above, flinging himself down the stairs with all the abandon and urgency of a man trying to out-run the devil. Only there was no one following him.

"Johnny?" Michael called, but the man took no notice of him. He whipped past Michael, streaking through the entryway and into the darkness of the ballroom.

Michael didn't have time to think. The pitcher he held crashed to the hardwood floor. He reached the ballroom in time to see Johnny fling open the doors and dive into the swirling storm outside. There was no choice but to follow him.

Outside, the wind assailed him with snow, stinging like needles in Michael's face and penetrating his clothing like it was made of fish netting. He couldn't see beyond a few feet. His flashlight was unable to slice through the thick atmosphere. Michael pushed forward anyway, following the rapidly filling footprints.

"Johnny! Johnny!"

The wind shifted then and he spotted his quarry, moving like a man possessed. He was heading for the stairs that led down to the dock.

What is he doing?

"Johnny!"

He had to stop him.

Unlike Johnny, Michael was a runner, slim, trim, and the captain of the track team, both in college and in high school. Despite the snow and ice underfoot, he closed the distance, still calling Johnny's name. Johnny never responded, never even twitched.

Not, at least, until Michael tackled him.

He hit him in the midsection, catching him off guard and knocking him sideways. They landed in a tangle of arms and legs. Michael managed to get on top and pin the taller man down. Johnny fought desperately and Michael's sore arm throbbed with the effort, but he held Johnny in place until his thrashing slowed and changed.

"Johnny?"

He got a growl in response, "Get off of me!"

It was a natural sound and Michael rolled off, relieved. Johnny's head came up, spitting snow.

"What's the idea?" he shouted.

"You tell me!" Michael responded, rubbing his arm. "Let's get inside before we get frostbite."

They made it back into the house, leaving the wind to beat futilely against the door after them. The girls were in the entryway, bent over the broken glass. Michael, knowing they only had a moment before the women saw them, grabbed Johnny by the collar and yanked him close.

"Quickly," he said. "What was that all about? Do you have a death wish or something?"

Johnny's eyes glinted in the beam of the flashlight and Michael regretted his words almost as soon as he said them. Johnny didn't look mad or crazy — it was worse than that. He looked terrified.

"I don't *know*." Johnny's voice cracked. "One minute I was up in that... room. Then I was outside, running for the dock, the water. I was so angry I could have killed someone. If you hadn't tackled me - Michael, it was like – like I was someone else..."

He broke off when Susan came into the room, holding a candle. Her golden hair caught the flame-light and gave the appearance of a halo, but her expression was too worried to be called saintly. Linda came in behind her, rubbing her arms and looking worried.

"What's going on?" Susan demanded. "Were you two outside? Did you hear something?"

Michael hesitated. What *had* happened to Johnny? What in his memory would send him running pell-mell through a snow-storm to reach the dock? Had he just snapped? If so, was he dangerous? Michael didn't know much about Johnny's condition, just what he heard from Susan, in whom Linda confided. Even then Linda only knew what Johnny would tell her and it was unlikely that Johnny would confess the true depth of his problem.

If he was dangerous, how could Michael control him and keep the others safe?

He didn't have to answer Susan. Johnny spoke up for him.

"Just an impulse," he said. He was shivering, the snow melting into his shirt. "The closed space was starting to get to me."

He left the room, brushing by Linda, who followed him. Susan stayed, arms folded, waiting. No one believed Johnny's obvious lie, but Michael didn't know what to say. He put his arm around Susan. She shuddered at the touch of his cold, wet sleeve.

"What happened, Michael?" she whispered.

He never could lie to her. He didn't even try now.

"I don't know. He was running for the dock, but he doesn't know why."

"Michael!"

She sounded frightened and he squeezed her close.

"We'll watch him," he said, in a tone that was meant to be reassuring. "It'll be okay, Susie. You'll see."

If only he could believe that himself.

CHAPTER 19

Linda left the living room so that Johnny and Michael could change out of their wet clothes in front of the fireplace. In the entryway, she watched as Susan swept the broken glassware into a paper bag.

"I feel bad about the pitcher," Linda said. "I wonder if it was valuable."

"If it was," Susan remarked, "it wouldn't have been left behind."

Linda went into the kitchen and butler's pantry to see if she could find another pitcher and more glasses. There were a few mismatched ones in a lonely cabinet. She found a towel and was wiping the glasses by candlelight, worrying about Johnny when she heard it: the sound of small feet running along the hallway overhead.

She froze. When she heard voices, she relaxed. *The boys went upstairs again, that's all.*

Nevertheless, her peace of mind was shattered. Looking around the dimly lit room, she began to think that maybe she was not alone. A whisper of movement in the corner, movement that could have easily been a draft or her own imagination, frightened her.

There is no such thing as spirits, she chided herself, only to ask, *If there aren't, then who bumped into you in the hallway?*

When she went back into the living room, the other three were there. No one looked as though they had just been running down halls.

Dinner was awkward. All they had to eat were the finger foods that Susan and Linda had prepared for the Christmas Eve party: little sausage rolls, cheese spread and crackers, chocolate chip cookies, Linda's first attempt at fruit cake, and a few bottles of wine. Michael brought in some more snow to melt by the fire for Susan, who refused to drink any of the liquor.

They did not talk much during their meal. Susan ate steadily, precisely, and twice as much as normal. Linda attributed this to both her pregnancy and the late hour. Michael ate well, complimenting Linda on her desserts and Susan for her appetizers. His cheer felt forced and his praise too fervent. Johnny played with his food and was silent. When asked, he claimed to be fine, but he was distant. He ate only when Linda reminded him to and stared morosely into the fire, clutching a blanket around his shoulders.

Linda was not interested in food, but she forced herself to eat anyway. When the creaks of the house grew too loud to be ignored, she began to talk, loosely and loudly. It was partially an attempt to draw the others out of their reverie, to join Michael in a pretense of normalcy, but mostly she spoke so she would not hear little feet running in the hall or disembodied giggles. Believing in hauntings was more difficult when you weren't hear things.

Despite her better judgement, she found herself asking Michael about the Reynolds family. Perhaps Michael understood, or perhaps he was trying to avoid listening, too. Whatever the reason, he was eager to speak about the family history, and soon drew Susan and Johnny into the discussion.

"No one knows why Grandfather Lionel took Jacob North in," Michael admitted. "Lionel had very old fashion views about pedigree and he wasn't the sort of man to take in a child out of sentiment. He never fully adopted Jacob, which is why his surname is still North. The most likely story suggests that Jacob is the offspring of Lionel's run-around son, Jasper, who died without leaving any legitimate heir."

"Lionel wouldn't acknowledge Jacob as his grandson?" Linda asked.

"There's nothing to prove he is," he replied. "In any case, as far as the company went, it wouldn't have changed anything. Lionel made it clear he would leave the business to his eldest son, Charles' father. When he died in a car accident, Charles was declared the new heir. They used to spend summers here, you know," he said, looking at Susan. "Charles, Jacob, and Irene."

"Did they?" she asked absently.

"Yes, when they were little. Irene lived here full time with her mother, the housekeeper. Charles stayed with his parents in Cambridge until their deaths. After that he and Jacob were in boarding schools for most of the year. It was, I gather, a rather severe life for the little boys, although probably better than the orphanage Jacob was found in."

I wouldn't bet on it, Linda thought.

Aloud, she asked, "So they knew Rachel Reynolds pretty well then? Coming up here every summer?"

"Rachel was the favorite aunt." Michael spoke around a mouthful of fruitcake.

"It must have been rough for Jacob during the war, hearing about Charles' exploits while he was stuck every day in a small office where everybody knew his story."

"Yeah, I guess. Still, he did all right. He ended up with the company in the end."

"I wonder if he found it difficult to pray for Charles' safe return," Susan said. "Working his brains out to keep the business going just so he can hand it over when Charles returned. It was terribly unfair. There must have been days when he wished Charles wouldn't come back at all. I know I would have."

"Oh, Susan!" Linda said, but Michael shrugged.

"Jacob had already made other plans," he said. "He got a good offer from General Motors and planned to transfer as soon as Charles was ready to take over. If it weren't for...Well, what happened, he wouldn't have even been part of RDC."

Susan shivered and moved closer to the fireplace.

Johnny cleared his throat. "It must have been an awful Christmas for them," he said.

Michael, who was staring hollow-eyed at his wife, responded, "Yes, it must have been. It was a triple tragedy. Not only did Charles kill his wife, but he also killed their child. Terrible."

"I keep forgetting Helene was pregnant," Linda mused. "Did Irene and Jacob have any children?"

He nodded. "A boy, William."

"A royal pain in the you-know-where," Susan added.

"Oh?" Linda queried.

"He's the heir apparent. Got the best of everything, never had to share, expected to be worth millions one day. Why wouldn't he turn out to be a brat?"

"He's not that bad," Michael protested.

"That's not what you said last year, when his highness was interning during summer vacation." Susan turned to Linda. "He worked as an office boy for Michael's department. Worked, that is, when he wasn't too busy riding horses or sailing around Nantucket Bay with his girlfriends."

"He's young and high-spirited," Michael said.

"Maybe," she sniffed. "All I know is a bright young man in the accounting department told me the company wouldn't last two years under William's administration."

"Are there plans for him to take over?" Linda asked.

Michael answered, "It's no secret that the board is pressuring Jacob to retire and let the company go public. The idea is to let new blood and ideas into the company, possibly leading to expansion, and to ensure the whole ship won't go down because of... potential poor leadership. But Jacob wants William to take over as president and he's determined to stay put until his son is old enough to take over. No one can talk him out of it."

"What did Rachel think?" Johnny asked suddenly.

His voice, so long absent from their conversation, was startling and every gaze turned to him. He had not moved or even twitched in the past few minutes, except to rub his right hand as though it were in pain. He didn't acknowledge their stares. He simply continued looking into the fire.

"Rachel probably wouldn't side with Jacob," Michael said after a minute. "She's been suspicious of him ever since he married Irene. Of course, keeping the company in the hands of North men would be to Irene's advantage."

"It's so medieval," Linda said.

"It was Lionel's company. He had the right to leave it to whomever he pleased. And Jacob North is a good president, or rather he was. Now the board thinks he's slowing down and becoming too cautious. In the end, though, it's still his company, fair and square."

"Would you look at this," Susan breathed suddenly.

She was sitting near the fire, her legs neatly folded beneath her so her short skirt perfectly covered everything. She had been sifting mindlessly through the pile of Rachel's research and now held a single sheet of lined paper. Linda went to look over her shoulder. The page was covered in methodical, if not exactly neat print, by a shaky hand.

"What is it?" Michael asked.

Susan read the title out loud: 'Murder Time-Line.'

That got their attention and now Michael and Johnny came over to take a look.

Murder Time-Line:

6:30pm: Guests start to arrive. Present: Helene, Irene, Lionel, Rachel

7:00pm: Charles arrives very upset. Irene says she hears him and Helene arguing.

7:30pm: Dinner, band sets up. Charles comes down, still pale. Irene asks him about his medication in front of everyone. Both Charles and Helene upset.

9:00pm: Helene goes to bed – headache she says.

9:10pm: Lionel says he spoke with Charles – they were going to meet in the morning.

10:00pm: Charles drinking too much – Lionel, too.

10:30pm: Jacob finally arrives. Lionel announces him at party. Jacob tries to speak with Charles, but Charles refuses coldly. Jacob and Irene go off together, then come back to the party and dance. I thought she was getting above her station, but didn't know she was engaged at the time.

11:10pm: Charles goes outside for a smoke.

11:15pm: Irene and Sheila take medicine to Helene.

11:20pm: Irene returns and tells me she's worried about Helene.

11:35pm: Call comes in for Jacob. He goes into study.

11:45pm: Charles comes in. He's thoroughly drunk now. Irene sends him upstairs to check on Helene.

Midnight: Charles appears. Charles runs outside. Jacob, already outside, follows him. Tragedy.

Note: Lionel in ballroom the whole time, Thomas in Exeter at family party.

"Who's Thomas?" Linda asked.

"The man they thought Helene was having the affair with," Michael said. "This time-line doesn't give any new information, does it?"

"Except that it indicates that Rachel didn't like Irene, even then," Johnny pointed out.

"It was written later," Susan said. "She could have been putting her current feelings on paper. But more likely you are right. It's hard to imagine she would have liked someone who was trying to marry up."

"She liked Helene well enough," Johnny said. "Why would she leave all of this behind?"

"She'd had a nervous breakdown after Irene's death," Michael said. "Maybe her caregivers thought it was better to leave it here, where she couldn't see it and be tortured by it."

"Look, there are pages and pages of the same thing!" Linda exclaimed.

Without speaking, they spread the timelines out on the floor, until nearly half the open space was covered in worn, scrawled pages, each almost exactly alike. All bore the title Murder Time-Line, contained matching dates and times, and were covered in the same handwriting in varying stages of deterioration. Some had more details, others less: but the varying players were cued at the same time and no new players were introduced. It was simply the same information, over and over again, as though Rachel, in her declining years, was trying to commit the facts to memory by studious repetition.

"No wonder people think she's obsessed," Linda said. "Think of the hours she must have spent, writing this over and over, and with arthritis, to boot."

"Something wasn't sitting right with her." Johnny mused.

"Something wasn't right with her." Susan corrected firmly.

As though in agreement, one of the shutters slammed against the outside wall of the living room, the sound reverberating like a gunshot. Susan squeaked in astonishment, jumping to her feet. Johnny swore and Michael muttered something under his breath, but the wind merely moaned in reply.

I hear you, Linda thought and shivered. She began to collect up the pages of research again, trying to ignore how her hands shook.

"It must be getting late," she said. "What time is it, Mike?"

Michael held his watch out to make use of the light from the fireplace. "Nine o'clock on December the 23rd," he intoned.

Susan, standing by the fire with one hand on her stomach and her eyes dreamy, said, "Helene is in bed and Jacob is on his way home."

Linda looked at Michael. He was uneasy and seemed about to say something. But it was Johnny who broke the silence.

"If Charles had a razor in his hand," he said. "Why did he run all the way down to the river to commit suicide?"

CHAPTER 20

This is going to go down in history as quite possibly the worst Christmas ever celebrated in America, Linda thought.

The conversation after Johnny's question, never particularly cheerful, had turned taciturn and positively morbid until it petered out altogether. Johnny sat huddled on the couch while Susan stood gazing at the fire with unblinking eyes. Linda and Michael picked at the food and watched the other two with undisguised anxiety.

Even in a well-lit room with a cheery warm fire, Linda could not shake the chill that had settled in her bones. She was stiff from watching, waiting, and listening – it was as though she were on the alert. Perhaps everyone was. Certainly they all jumped whenever a shutter slammed or the house creaked over the wind.

We are acting like children, she thought. *Like children who've been spooked by their own campfire stories.*

She regretted ever finding Rachel's research. It had only aggravated the tension and her obsessive lists, made out in that consistently deteriorating hand, were enough to get under Linda's skin.

The old lady was insane. That's why the room was left the same. That's the only reason why. Only an insane person would let another insane person frighten them.

It was not as comforting a thought as she had hoped.

Finally, Michael had enough of the silence. He hopped up from the floor.

"Oh, come on, guys," he said, collecting the dishes with vigor, "it's Christmas after all. What do you say to some games or a sing-along?"

Even Linda had difficulty faking enthusiasm, but they all went along with it. Susan helped pack up the little remaining food while Johnny moodily poked the fire and Linda helped Michael with the dishes, wiping them and hauling them back into the kitchen.

"I don't know where you found these," Michael said, "so I'll leave you to put them away while I help Johnny with the firewood."

Though Linda did not relish spending time alone in the near-darkness, she was not about to tell Michael that she was afraid. Instead, she worked swiftly, ignoring the tremor in her hands and the feeling of ice in her spine. She tried not to listen too hard, afraid she would hear the patter of little feet where there should be none.

That was when she heard *it*...

She stopped dead, one hand on the shelf with the platter that she had just replaced, the other wrapped protectively around the candlestick.

The sound was faint at first, but grew until Linda could almost make out the tune, '*I'll be Home for Christmas.*'

There was no vocal accompaniment. The notes, singular and dull, had no resonance or warmth and slipped through the air like mist. It was a bone-chilling melody that did not belong.

It's that music box, Linda thought. *Susan must have brought it down with her.*

She had nearly convinced herself when the music began to swell. A bass and piano joined in while a sad clarinet played the melody. It played the verses, weeping into the night:

'I'll be home for Christmas... If only in my dreams...'

Sweetly, sickly, it ended, only to begin again. Linda found herself following the sound through the dining room and into the entryway, where she stopped. The sound was louder, but wavering, as though losing radio signal. It was not coming from the living room. It was coming from the ballroom. And there was a light under the door.

Oh God, oh God, oh God-

"Linda?"

Linda whirled around. Johnny's form was a black stain against the far wall of the staircase and she was never so relieved to see anyone in her life.

She ran to the foot of the stairs. "Do you hear that?" she asked breathlessly.

The light from her candle made his eyes deep caverns in his face. She realized, then, that though he was poised to go up the stairs, he carried no candle of his own.

"Hear what?" he asked.

The music had stopped. The air was still. The only sound was the minute sputtering of her candle and the faint whispers of Michael and Susan in the living room. The ever-present wind roared like static noise above everything.

"There was music," Linda said. "And a light-"

When she gestured to the broad double doors, everything was dark.

"It was there!" she said. "I *saw* it."

"Linda, I was here," he said. "There was no music and there was no light."

"Then what *did* I hear?" she demanded.

She wanted to shout, "I am *not* going crazy!", but long months of living with her post-combat brother in varying stages of therapy and collapse kept the word from her lips.

Johnny shrugged. "There was nothing, Linda. I would have seen it."

He had to be right. The music had been too loud and contrasted too strongly with the wind and the deathly silence shrouding the rest of the house for him to miss. If he had been standing on that staircase he would have heard it. Unless...

Johnny hadn't moved from his position on the stairs. She could see his hand gripping the banister as though he were afraid of falling. His whole body was rigid and tense, ready to run.

She lifted the candle higher to illuminate his face. He blinked.

"What *are* you doing there, Johnny?" she asked.

Johnny hesitated, glancing up at the landing. Then he looked at his hand on the banister and with an effort released his grip. "I don't know," he replied sheepishly. "I wanted to stretch my legs. The living room is feeling a little small right now."

"So you were going upstairs without a light?"

Johnny glared at her. "Let's go back to the others. I need a drink." He brushed past her, hurrying into the living room without a backward glance.

Now Linda hesitated. She lifted her candle to view the landing, then the ballroom doors. There was no music, no sound, no light, and no movement. There was nothing to see.

As she joined the others in the living room, she wondered why she was not more relieved.

CHAPTER 21

No one wanted to sleep. Michael suggested whist to pass the time. Michael and Susan partnered against Linda and Johnny. They played for about an hour, everyone making a conscious effort to keep the conversation light. Johnny uncorked another bottle of wine and drank half of it himself, gulping down the aromatic liquid. Drinking made Johnny even less talkative, but as he seemed to be relaxing, neither Michael nor Linda objected. Michael offered everyone a cigarette, but found no takers. He smoked his way through half the pack.

Finally, after about an hour, Susan abruptly laid her cards down and yawned.

"I'm tired," she said. "I think I'm going to turn in."

With that, the game was over. Linda gave Johnny the remainder of her wine to drink. She gathered up the glasses and put away the cards. Johnny slurred "Good night and Merry Christmas," before stumbling over to a spot on the floor with a blanket. He was asleep in seconds.

Michael positively refused to let Susan go back upstairs.

"It's too cold up there," he said. "I won't have my wife freeze to death on our first Christmas together."

Susan allowed him and Linda to set up the couch for her. No one considered changing into their pajamas. The fire was only barely managing to keep the cold at bay. Susan used her coat as a blanket, lying obediently down on the couch under Michael's direction.

Michael was exhausted. It had come on suddenly, only moments before Susan had broken up the game. He fought to keep his eyes open as he tucked his wife into her makeshift bed. His arms felt leaden, his head ached, and his face was still raw from the wind.

He was tucking the blanket around Susan, stroking her head and murmuring "Goodnight, sweetheart," when she reached out and grabbed his hand with both of hers.

"Michael," she hissed. "What time is it?"

She whispered low so that Linda, now across the room, couldn't hear.

Michael consulted his watch, tilting his wrist so that he could see the arms by the firelight. "Almost ten-thirty," he said, barely containing his yawn.

She relaxed, sinking back down into the couch.

"Ten-thirty," she breathed. "Then there's still time."

Michael frowned. "Time? Time for what?"

She did not answer. Her eyes were closed and her breathing was deep and even. Susan had fallen asleep.

He watched her for a moment, taking in the lines of her face and the beauty of her form. He traced her face gently with the back of his hand. She never stirred. She was a beautiful girl and, until tonight, a tower of strength as well.

I hope she sleeps. Poor thing had more than her fair share of scares today. She must be exhausted to fall asleep so quickly after her nap this afternoon.

Linda was sitting in front of the fire at the end of her make-shift bed, her arms wrapped around her knees. Her lips moved silently in prayer and there was a rosary in her clenched hands. She rocked unconsciously, shifting her gaze to Johnny every so often.

Michael sent up his own prayer of thanksgiving for shelter from the storm, before setting up his own bed in front of Susan's couch. He was so tired he could have slept on bare floor. The blanket he lay down first offered so little padding he might well have.

He was too tired to care. Sleep rolled over him like a wave, drawing him out to sea. The last thing he saw before succumbing to exhaustion was Linda sitting before the fireplace, pouring her heart out silently to a string of wooden beads.

Part Three:
CONFRONTATION

CHAPTER 22

He was in the jungle again. The heat was bad enough, but the humidity was like adding an extra fifty pounds to his pack. Sweat poured off his body in an unceasing torrent until his uniform was soaked and his boots slick and heavy.

The scouting platoon moved silently through the trees, or at least as silently as could be managed while carrying gear and weaponry. This area of the territory was in US control; safe the brass said, secured, the newspapers said. Johnny knew better and so did the others. To assume you were alone was foolhardy at best.

Scott walked alongside, his normally jovial face a mask of tension. Scott was never the type to worry about little things like death. *"We're here until we aren't anymore, Johnny my boy. No use in worrying about what you can't change."* But today he must have had a premonition of what was about to happen, for his cheery blue eyes were worried and he spoke only when spoken too.

"Something's wrong," he muttered whenever Johnny came close. "I don't like it. I just don't like it."

Johnny knew what was coming. He had been there before, caught in that odd space of being trapped in a dream and knowing it. He desperately tried to warn Scott. He turned to him again and again to speak. His lips moved but no sound came out. Scott, scanning the impenetrable jungle, didn't even notice.

Johnny screamed silently, *"Wake up, wake up, I don't want to live through this again!"*

But the trap was sprung.

It happened in slow motion. Shots were fired. Men screamed and knives flashed. Scott was hit. He fell down, eyes wide with shock and his mouth twisted in agony. Johnny could not tell the difference between his company and the enemy. It was all blood, sweat, pain, and the sure knowledge that the only thing between him and his own death was someone else's.

The explosion came out of nowhere.

It caught Johnny on his right and flung him into the trunk of a nearby tree. The impact was shattering. He lay insensible but conscious, looking up at the sky through the pine trees.

That never happened...

The dream shifted. He was waking up on a wooden pallet in a bare cabin. Sleep was thick and he was clumsy. He fell off the bed onto the hard-packed, dirt floor. When he tried to catch himself with his right hand, he collapsed, rolling onto his back, disoriented. His breath was coming out in cold clouds. From outside the hut came the sound of heavy tramping boots and guttural shouts of *"Aufmerksamkeit! Aufmerksamkeit!"*

He thought, *They've caught me. Oh God, they've caught me.*

His vision went black, then green. He was back in the jungle, walking next to Scott. Only this time Johnny's right sleeve was pinned up, empty to his shoulder. He was thinking, *When they come, I won't be able to fire...*

He was right.

Over and over the dream played out with different variations until Johnny was finally able to wrench himself out of it, panting. He was not in the jungle. He was in the living room, so close to the fire that it was singeing his back. He rolled away and sat up, trying to catch his breath. He was coated in sweat and shook like he had a fever. He looked at his hands and was profoundly relieved when he saw that he still had both.

It was only a dream. Just a nightmare.

Linda slumbered peacefully next to him, her hair glinting red in the dying firelight. Susan was a draped shadow on the couch and Michael lay curled up on the floor at the head of the couch. No one stirred. He was alone in the cold winter night.

Rather than subsiding, the storm was gaining power. The house creaked and settled under its influence. For the first time, Johnny wondered how much structural damage there would be. He was glad for the shutters although they increased the feeling of isolation in the house.

He was too nervous to sleep again and wondered what time it was. There was no way to check short of looking at Michael's watch. Johnny never wore one himself, not since…

No need to go there, man.

He kicked the blanket off impatiently and stood. If he sat there, doing nothing, his imagination was going to run wild, inviting another panic attack. There was nothing else to do but walk until the nightmares faded away. Walk until he was too tired for anything else but sleep. Walk until the noise and isolation stopped making him feel he was being watched by hostile forces…

He got to his feet. He had not removed his shoes before sleeping, an old military habit he couldn't shake. He grabbed the candlestick. It took him three tries before he was able to light it.

He was still shaking and his right hand felt curiously weak. He ignored it and left the living room. He could not pace in there without waking the others up and then there would be the usual rounds of questions, *"Are you all right? Another of your episodes? Can I get you something?"* Like he was just a damn cripple his overworked sister had to nurse once she was finished looking after all her other patients.

Crippled and useless, a shell of a man. Charlie might as well have killed me. It would be better than living as I am — like a ghost among the living.

Johnny had not intended to go upstairs. He had a vague notion of pacing in the entryway, in front of the ballroom where he had noticed before that the floorboards did not creak. He was so wrapped in thought, so miserably intent on working through the significance of the dream, that he did not pay attention until reaching the top of the stairs.

He stopped there, surprised at himself.

This isn't the time to go poking around, Johnny…

That was when he heard footsteps.

His mouth went dry. The steps came from the end of the hall, so thickly shrouded in shadow that he could make out no movement. But he heard it for certain, the slow, dull thud of a man's shoe on creaking floorboards.

He was not alone.

I knew it…

He snuffed out the light immediately. Darkness fell hard and heavy upon him. The footsteps grew louder, made bold by the lack of light. They were traveling away from Johnny, shuffling as though walking was difficult. Helene's door opened, then shut again, gently, apparently of its own accord.

He's trapped, Johnny thought. *There's no other way out of that room.*

It never occurred to him to go get the others. He plunged forward, holding out one hand to feel along the walls and using the other to pull his folding knife out of his back pocket. It was one of the few souvenirs that he had kept from his stint in the army, a black, serviceable knife with no frills and few attachments. But the blade was sharp and clean as a razor's edge. Johnny made sure of that, polishing and sharpening it every week, until even he worried that he was obsessing.

Darkness closed in around him. He could hear nothing of the intruder, nothing but the wind and the rustling sound of his own clothes as he moved slowly down the hallway. His hand dragged along the rough wallpaper, touching wood grain and dried patches of wallpaper paste. He was certain that someone was there. His senses were on fire. It was as though he could almost smell the other person.

He reached Helene's door at last. He grasped the knob and the door gave a little. It had not been closed all the way by the intruder.

Johnny snapped the blade of his knife open, wincing at the small sharp sound. He stood in the doorway, listening.

Nothing.

There were no footsteps, no rustling noise, not a sound, but there was a presence. Johnny felt it, could almost *see* him through the door.

He pushed the door open, holding his knife at the ready. The door swung easily enough. If there was a slight creak from the hinges, that need not alarm the intruder; the house was creaking like mad under the pressure of the wind.

Johnny stepped into the room.

It was like going blind. He stood in absolute darkness, every sense on overdrive, his eyes straining, looking for a glimmer of light. There was nothing, nothing but him standing a few steps within the doorway with his knife at the ready... and it, the person standing somewhere in the shadows.

They waited. They watched. Neither spoke, neither breathed.

Then the intruder sighed.

Johnny moved like an arrow released from its string; sharp, smooth, fast, sure. It was as he moved, as he put himself where he could not retreat, that it occurred to him that this was a trap-and he was walking right into it.

CHAPTER 23

Linda sat up with a gasp, wide-awake and heart pounding. The wind roared, snuffing out the cheery sounds of a dance music, echoing faintly through the empty entryway.

It had *sounded* like swing music, but that couldn't be.

I must have been dreaming.

But nonetheless, something *had* awakened her...

She was in the living room, stretched out before the fireplace as she had been when she went to sleep. Judging by the fire, Linda had not been asleep all that long. Michael and Susan were still sleeping where she'd last seen them, though Michael had shifted, curling up in a ball on the floor by the head of the couch.

Johnny was gone. His blanket lay crumpled up dangerously near the flames. She leaned forward and pulled it away with a shaking hand.

It was just a dream, she told herself. *Just a nightmare. Johnny woke you when he left...*

Then it came again; swing music, happy and lively and somehow hollow, as though it were only an echo. It poured in through the open doorway of the living room, seeping into Linda's very skin, leaving it cold to the touch. This time, a voice accompanied it,

"Should old acquaintance be forgotten

"and never brought to mind?"

It had to be her imagination. It *had* to be! Linda sat with the blanket around her shoulders, shivering and listening, wishing that Johnny would come back and that the sound would just die away. It did not and he did not.

"For auld lang syne, my dear,

"for auld lang syne!"

Perhaps there was a radio somewhere in the house, one with a faulty wire or something. Perhaps it was a broadcast she was listening to. Nothing frightening in that. Though if there was a radio, then there would be news broadcasting as well...

"We'll take a cup of kindness yet..."

"In the days of auld lang syne..."

I am *hearing this.*

She was up on her feet before she had finished the thought. Even Johnny could not deny it this time. Perhaps he was already out there investigating. Whatever he was doing, Linda intended to find out the truth about the music, this time *before* someone could persuade her otherwise.

Like Johnny, it didn't occur to her to wake the others. It was a decision they both would come to regret.

Gathering the blanket around her shoulders, she went out into the entryway. The music did not change. It did not grow louder or softer or sound nearer when she went to it. Rather, it seemed to travel with her into the other room, sitting distractedly just beyond where she could locate its source.

Not that it mattered much, because there was something else to draw her attention. The ballroom doors were open...and light was pouring out of the room.

This was not the warm flickering glow of a few candles and a fireplace. It was full light, pale and unchanging, like the moon on a clear winter's night. It was too pale to be electrical light, at least not any electrical light that Linda had ever seen. With the storm raging outside, it could not be moonlight.

The music died away and this time she heard clapping, polite and encouraging, like people would at a party in front of a live band.

The music started again, *'I'll be Home for Christmas'*, accompanied by a mournful clarinet. Now Linda could clearly pinpoint its origin. It came from the ballroom.

This is impossible, she thought.

There was only one way to be sure.

Linda walked into the ballroom.

It was like stepping into a freezer. The music gained in volume. Now it sounded like there was a band playing at the far end of the room, away from the double fireplaces. There were other sounds, too: polite chatter, laughter, and the swishing of wide skirts. The room was empty...but it was alive.

As Linda stood there, something brushed by her shoulder, exactly like a person being swung about by partner on a dance floor. But it was the giggle that followed that broke her nerve.

Linda gasped and whirled around to run, but before she could take a step, the ballroom doors swung shut. She launched herself against them. They were locked. The wooden doors might as well have been brick and iron for all the impression her pounding and pushing made. The music and voices grew louder, until she could distinguish conversations and hear the click of heels on wooden floors. Someone touched her shoulder and she screamed for Johnny but there was no answer.

She turned around, pressing her back against the wood panels. The sound was growing. She could smell cigarettes and perfume and spiced apple cider. The light was beginning to play tricks on her, bending and blending until she could almost make out shapes and figures, figures dancing and talking and laughing, figures that could not possibly be there.

The butler's pantry.

Suddenly, she remembered the other door. Loosening her grip on the door handle, she raced through the room, through the unnatural light, through the bodies that were not there, to the door at the far side of the room, the door that led to the kitchen and sanity. But when she reached it, it was locked and as solid as the double doors.

She screamed, pounding on the wooden panels, shouting for Johnny, Michael, and Susan. No one heard her. No one could hear her.

Johnny didn't hear the music before. He and Susan and Michael can't hear it now. Only I am hearing this, seeing this. I'm losing my mind. I'm trapped in here and I'm losing my mind.

Linda gave up, leaning against the door, burying her face so she could not see.

It's a nightmare, Linda. A nightmare – you'll wake up.

But she did not. The voices grew in volume. Someone asked for more punch. Another wheeled his partner into another dance. Someone placed their hands on Linda's shoulders. When she screamed, he only laughed as though she had said something flirtatious. Then she was being led away from the door on legs that were not her own. She was dancing, whirling amid the light and shadows and the music that should not be there, her own laughter drowning out her screams for help.

CHAPTER 24

Susan was running down the hall, her hair loose and falling into her eyes, her robe flapping behind her, it's belt threatening to trip her. Her lungs burned. She was screaming, a long, primal, terrified scream that no one heard but the being that followed her.

"Stop – stop, stay away from me!"

She was at the stairs, she was flying down them. The being wouldn't stop. It wouldn't leave her alone, it would catch her. Even now it was reaching out for her, hands brushing against her hair. She raised her fists to ward it off.

"Don't touch me, don't touch me!"

Then she was falling. The ground was rushing up, yet it took forever to reach her, and when it did, she would die. She knew this, as surely as she knew the voice that kept calling out to her, over and over again: *"Why? Why? Tell me why?"*

But she was beyond answering...

***

Susan awoke with a start. The room was in utter stillness except for the crackle of the fire and the rush of the wind around the eaves. For a moment, she did not know where she was. When she reached out and found that Michael was not next to her, she panicked. It was only when she touched the back of the couch that she remembered.

She was not home. She was in the old Reynolds house, waiting out a blizzard with Michael and their friends. They were alone and isolated and she'd had another dream.

That in itself was peculiar. Susan rarely dreamt and never had nightmares, yet today she'd had several. This last was the most chilling of all. She had been Irene North, tearing down the staircase like a demon was chasing her, losing her footing, falling, dying...

Susan shook her head and swung her legs around to drop over the side of the couch. The floor was cold to the touch, the chill soaking through her unfashionably thick socks as she stood up.

Michael was curled up on the floor, deeply asleep. Linda and Johnny were gone. After that dream, Susan did not relish the idea of being alone, even briefly, but she didn't want to wake Michael. She pulled a blanket around her shoulders and moved towards the entryway door to go look for the others who were already awake.

She had hardly gone a step when she heard a creaking behind her, like a door opening.

In all the excitement and distractions of the discoveries earlier, she had almost forgotten about the den where Linda had found Rachel's research in the old desk. They had closed the door when they left. It stood open now and there was a faint light like the pale beam of a flashlight emitting from the doorway.

"Linda?"

There was no answer but the light shifted as though whoever was in the room was moving about.

Probably looking for a book, Susan thought.

She picked up the flashlight that stood on the end table by the couch and went into the den.

When she stepped inside the room, the light went out. There was a grinding sound, like wood moving over wood. When she snapped on her flashlight, the room was empty.

Susan frowned and pulled the blanket more tightly about her shoulders. There was no other way out, except by the windows which remained boarded, or through the door which she was blocking.

"Linda?" she called, playing her light around the room. "Johnny?"

No one answered of course. There was no one there. Even though the wind was playing tricks on her ears and making it *sound* like there was someone tip-toeing through the room, she could see very plainly that the room was empty.

Susan turned to go. She wanted to run, but she had never run from shadows and she would not do so now.

There was another sound, and she whipped her light around. A small black book balanced on the edge of a bookshelf, teetering as she watched. Then it fell.

Susan's heart caught in her throat. She threw the light all around the room. There was nothing, no one, no hand that had moved the book, no one scrambling behind the desk. Then, slowly, she dropped the light down towards the book.

It was lying on the floor, a small thing, as big as her hand and not thick. It was worn, though the pages seemed tight. There was no print on the cover, but she recognized it as belonging to the set of Shakespeare plays that she'd seen earlier that day.

Susan flicked the light around the room once more and then looked back at the book. It seemed to be waiting for her to pick it up. She did not want to leave the doorway.

It's only a room. There's no one in it. You saw that!

Slowly, she took a step towards the book, then another. She reached out slowly and just as her hand touched the book's cover, a woman screamed.

The sound erupted from over Susan's head, so loud and so close that she fell to the floor, over the book, and rolled out of the way. Her back struck the desk and she looked up, bringing the light with her.

There was no one else in the room. The book was lying on the floor where she left it.

Shaking, she leaned forward to reach for it.

The book shot out of her grasp as violently as if someone had kicked it.

Susan screamed, lurching back. Her cry was outmatched by the woman's scream; long, twisted, maniacal. There was a rush and a roar and wind like icicles filled the room, swirling about, tugging at Susan's blanket, drenching her with cold.

Something snatched the stuffed chair and flung it at Susan. She had only just moved out of the way in time. It struck the desk and the force half turned it. Susan tumbled to the ground. The wind was blinding her, making her eyes water. Her hair pulled out of its bun. She struggled to push herself up from the floor but something struck her on the head sharply. She yelped and a book tumbled to the floor at her feet.

Susan looked up, bringing the flashlight with her. Through the wind-stung tears she saw that the shelves were swept clean, but the books were not on the floor — they were hovering several feet above her head, black covers spread like bat's wings. They wavered tremulously, waiting, watching, poised for attack.

She flicked the flashlight to the doorway. It was empty. She looked up at the books again, then at the door.

She moved, but she did not get very far.

CHAPTER 25

The scream yanked Michael out of a deep sleep. For a moment, he lay perfectly still, listening to the wind, wondering what he'd heard, waiting for it to sound again. His gaze drifted to the couch. It was empty.

When the noise came again it was much louder — it was Susan screaming.

Michael jumped up onto his feet, slipping when the blanket tangled around his legs. He regained balance only to lose it again when he collided with a chair, tripping and falling hard. As he fought to get up, Susan's screams came again, closer and more terrified. She was in the room beyond the living room.

He vaulted to his feet and threw himself through the doorway.

Michael stepped into a hurricane. The wind tore at his face and clothes and stabbed at his eyes, nearly blinding him. Susan was crying out painfully and he stumbled forward. A beam from the flashlight jerked around madly, like it was being used to ward off something.

"Susan!"

Something hard, but light, struck him in the face.

Susan shrieked, "I'm here! I'm here!"

The light steadied. He saw Susan on her knees, fighting off what he thought were huge bats. They were whirling about her, striking at her face and shoulders. A few broke off their attack to turn on him, striking at him with pointed edges.

They weren't bats. They were books.

He darted forward and grabbed Susan by the wrists, dragging her to her feet. Still screaming, she stumbled forward and they lurched towards the doorway. The bat-like things pulled back for a moment, but only to reassemble. When they attacked again, Michael had the door in his hand. He yanked it shut behind him.

The heavy oak door shivered under the assault but it held and the bat-books withdrew.

Michael sighed and looked at his wife. She was bent over, weeping silently with one hand pressed to her mouth. He took the flashlight out of her hand and she turned to him. She had blood on her cheek under her enormous eyes and she was shaking uncontrollably.

"What was that?" he demanded.

She whimpered. Michael pulled her into his arms and she shivered there. He could feel her heart beating through her chest, almost in unison with his own. He closed his eyes and pressed her closer to him. Then he realized…they were in the living room and they were alone.

He shone the beam of the flashlight over Linda's blankets, then Johnny's. He pulled away from Susan's embrace. "Where are Linda and Johnny?"

She shook her head.

It was then that they heard a dull, pounding sound echoing through the entryway and into the living room.

Michael did not stop to think. He headed out into the entryway with Susan hurrying close behind him.

The room was empty and for a moment he thought that he had misheard. Susan cowered behind him, so close that he could feel her breath on his shoulders. Neither noticed the light under the doorway of the ballroom and they were not permitted to hear anything but the storm outside.

Then the banging came again. Someone was beating on the front door.

Michael thought, *Why would they go outside?* He instantly answered his thought, *They wouldn't.*

"Don't open it," Susan whispered. She was leaning against him now, her hand groping until he placed his own in hers. "Please... don't..."

There was a voice now, and the pounding grew more desperate. The wind howled. Michael thought, *Whoever it is, they'll freeze to death if I don't let them in.*

The voice sounded human, even if the wind was so strong that it carried away the words. If there was anything Michael wanted to see right now, it was someone normal and human.

He stepped forward and wrenched open the door.

The door was old and reluctant to give. Years of underuse and the natural pattern of swelling and shrinking of the wood made it fit almost too well in the doorframe. It opened at last, relenting with a banshee's screech of wood-on-wood. Snow poured in, almost obscuring the large figure who barreled his way through the doorway and into the middle of the hallway.

"It's about time!" the figure shot at Michael in passing.

Michael should have been nervous, terrified even, after what had happened in the den. But this new intruder was a person — a man — definable and earthly. His boots made heavy clopping noises as he went past and his curses, difficult to hear over the wind, were reassuring. This man was made of the same flesh and bone as they were. As Michael looked at him, he was sure of that at least.

He pushed the door shut behind the visitor, beating back the wind and snow and slipping a little on the accumulation. His relief was tarnished with confusion. No one should have been out on a night like this.

Michael turned his flashlight on the visitor who stood in the middle of the entryway, beating the snow from his pants and muttering complaints. He was a tall man, made broader by the leather bomber jacket he wore and he moved with a swiftness that spoke of great energy. His dark hair was threaded through with white, although he did not look much more than a decade older than Michael himself. He was armed too – a thick black belt supported a holstered automatic.

When Michael saw that, his heart sank. He looked to Susan, standing in the middle of the room, one fist pressed tightly against her mouth while her other rested on her stomach. Her face was white and drawn. She looked as if she would be sick at any moment.

The stranger was not even looking at them.

"…could have frozen to death outside if you'd waited just a half-second longer to get your robes on," he was saying sarcastically. He ran a hand through his hair and turned sharp blue eyes to look at Michael. "Not that it's much better in here. Haven't you guys ever heard of a little thing called a furnace? Or is freezing to death some new age cult thing I haven't heard of yet?"

Then Michael saw the badge and he breathed in relief. "You're the police!" he said.

"One of them, anyway," he said. His accent was Northeastern, probably from New Hampshire, but there was a touch of New York in it too. "I saw your car on the side of the road, thought I'd check things out, see if you needed help… are you all right, ma'am?"

Susan was staring up at the balcony above them, wide-eyed and terrified. Her hand lifted to point and both men swung about. Michael flipped the beam of the flashlight upward but there was nothing up there except for the gently swaying chandelier.

Susan's sigh drew his attention back to the entryway. She had collapsed, limp, into the officer's arms. Michael gave an involuntary cry. The officer lifted her up and said, "Is there any place in this house that's warm?"

Michael gestured towards the living room and followed him in.

The fire had burned down somewhat. Michael, his hands shaking and his mind whirling, threw in a few pieces of wood and prodded it with the poker until the fire leapt to life again. Though the flame burned voraciously it did not seem to touch the cold that had settled into his bones. He could only hope that Susan was not feeling the same.

His arm ached anew, a dull pain that was somehow deeper than a bruise. He rubbed it absently and found himself talking. "We were in a car accident, the four of us. I didn't expect to see anyone else until the storm ended."

"The four of you?"

"Yes. Johnny and Linda are around here somewhere."

Where were they? Michael remembered the incident of Johnny outside on the deck and shivered involuntarily. If Johnny had tried that again — but Linda was with him, surely she could handle it. She was a nurse after all and Susan…

He looked over at the couch. The cop was kneeling beside Susan, checking her pulse. A few minutes ago the man had seemed like a gift from God, a touch of sanity in a world gone mad. Now, in the light of the fire, in that room that Susan had so carefully decorated just like Rachel had twenty-five years ago, his presence seemed suspect.

What is a cop doing out on a night like this? Michael wondered. *Is he even really here? Or is he another figment of my imagination? Like books that come to life to attack my wife? Am I going mad?*

His gaze drifted to his wife's battered face and his stomach clenched in anger. Imagination or not, something had put those marks there.

The policeman was studying Susan's face, his mouth tight. After a moment, he rose and turned towards Michael. His hand rested lightly on his pistol. He took a step forward, a ground eating step that meant business. Michael, standing there with the poker in his hand, watched him warily.

"What did she do, son?" The officer jabbed a thumb over his shoulder towards the sleeping woman. "Burn your dinner?"

It took Michael a moment to get his implication and when he did, horror very nearly took his speech away. "Now, wait a minute, that isn't what happened —I'm not — she-" Alarmed, Michael took a step forward.

The officer moved quickly, putting himself between Michael and the couch with a hand out to stop him.

"Take it easy, kid," he said. "Just calm down."

Michael froze. What could he say? That books had attacked them in the far room? That something was trying to kill them? How do you explain something that you can't explain, or see, or even truly believe in, yourself?

He looked at the officer and let his hands drop helplessly.

"You don't understand," he said.

The officer was watching him with hard eyes.

"Sure I understand," he said. "She tripped and fell while shaving. Happens all the time. Now, why don't you put that poker down and we'll talk about it. Where are your two friends? Or did they go for a walk, too?"

His hand tightened ever so slightly around the pistol grip.

Michael's mouth was dry. He opened it, forcing himself to speak. "I don't know where they are, but there's something – someone – in this house. Something that-"

Linda's scream ripped through the atmosphere.

Both men jumped.

"What the *hell*?" shouted the officer.

Michael was already running for the entryway.

The ballroom doors stood open now, unnatural light pouring through them. Michael stepped inside and was instantly overwhelmed. Cold air washed over him like an ice-bath. There was noise: music, chatter, and movement. The light dazzled him and he could feel bodies brushing up against him, murmuring to each other by his ear. All of them were gripped by the same sensation of terror.

When his eyes cleared, he saw Linda. She was standing in the middle of the room, glowing with an unnatural light. Her arms were suspended as though in a dance with another. Other beings jostled Michael's arm and whispered around him. All he could see of them were the faintest outlines, like shadows disappearing in new light.

But Linda was not the only one he could see in the room. Johnny was stalking towards his sister, his left arm raised over his head and blood coursing down his arm, a bloodied knife in his hand.

"Johnny!" Michael gasped.

Johnny did not flinch. He bore down on Linda, who remained frozen in place, her eyes wide and her mouth open in a mute sort of terror.

Michael darted forward, reaching Linda first. He pulled her behind him. She was as stiff and unyielding as Johnny's face was white and changed. He looked like a man possessed. He looked like a man about to kill.

Michael barely had a chance to react as the officer positioned himself between Michael and Johnny and brought his pistol to bear on the soldier.

"All right, sunshine," he snapped. "Drop it."

"Don't!" Michael shouted at the officer just as Linda gasped, "Charlie!"

Johnny stopped short, inches away from the officer, his eyes still riveted on Linda. There was blood on his face and shirt and more running down his arm. Except for where the knife bit into his trembling left hand, Michael could see no cut or abrasion.

Everything stopped in that moment. The shuffling of invisible feet, the audible gasp from unseen throats, the rustling of the Emperor's clothing. Time itself suspended – or maybe it had bridged with another night. Suddenly, Michael was aware of the scent of the perfumes and spices, an odor like that of bodies that have been mingling in a warm room. A clock ticked though althere was no clock in the room.

Johnny stood poised for the strike, teetering on the edge of sanity, threatening to take the rest of them down with him.

"Put it down, son," the officer demanded. "Put the knife down."

"Johnny," Michael ventured.

Johnny blinked. Tears rolled down his cheeks, mingling with sweat and drying blood. He looked around blankly, wobbling on legs that seemed suddenly too tall.

Michael thought, *He's overdosed. He doesn't know what he's doing.*

Linda shifted behind Michael, trying to step forward. He stopped her, gripping her arm to hold her in place. She resisted but then stopped trying.

"Charlie," she said again.

Johnny looked at her. The knife came down as the tears rolled faster and thicker.

"She's gone," he said hoarsely. "Oh God, she's gone!"

The invisible, impossible clock chimed twelve. Someone screamed but it was not a real cry like Susan's scream earlier. This one was hollow somehow, like a memory of a scream, terrifying and just beyond the here and now.

They all jumped, all but Johnny that is. He remained still. Only his gaze shifted. He was looking over them, now pointing with the knife out the window.

"*There!*" he said.

He was running towards the door before they could react.

The room exploded in a cacophony of sound – people shouting, crying, moving, shoving. Linda's cry of "*Johnny!*" and the officer's warning shout could barely be heard above everything else. The officer was turning, bringing his gun around to bear on the fleeing man.

Michael shoved Linda out of the way and brought his arm down on the gun hand. "Not that, not that!" Then he plunged through the doors and outside into the night and the swirling storm. "Johnny! Stop!"

It was only fractionally colder outside. Michael hardly noticed it anyhow. He could not see more than a few feet beyond his face. He knew from past experience where Johnny was heading – the dock and the icy river at the end of it.

He ran blindly, stumbling through shifting snow drifts and falling branches. From behind him, a flashlight shone, cutting weakly through the whirling flakes. It bounced around crazily and for a split second he saw Johnny's back as he weaved through the snow. He was several yards ahead, almost at the dock.

Michael pushed his legs harder. It was like running through a nightmare between the darkness and the sluggishness caused by the snow. Somehow, he cut the distance, but only just barely. His feet hit the wood of the dock which had been kept largely clear by the cutting wind. The flashlight beam caught Johnny's back again and Michael launched himself, slipping on the icy wood.

He caught Johnny on the small of the back and they both went down, smashing hard onto the frozen planks. His arm made contact with the dock and pain seared up into his shoulder. An elbow caught Michael in the stomach, knocking the breath out of him. Johnny thrashed about with his left arm, his legs kicking. He was crying something, too: "Why? Why? *Why?*"

Michael tried to pin him down, but Johnny overpowered him easily, flipping him over so Michael was against the dock with Johnny on top. The blade of the knife grazed his neck. Michael twisted, but Johnny's arm came down on his neck, pinning him to the boards, cutting off his oxygen.

"*Johnny,* it's *me!*" he gasped.

Johnny loomed over him sobbing. "*Why?*"

He pressed harder, bending over in grief. Michael's lungs were burning. Black spots erupted before his eyes. There was a shout over the storm. Johnny stopped to listen and Michael, with the strength of desperation, threw his shoulder over and toppled the man, throwing him off and over the side of the dock.

Johnny screamed. There was a cracking sound. Michael, coughing and sputtering, threw himself forward and caught Johnny's arm just before it disappeared under the ice. But he had no leverage and followed Johnny into the icy water below.

He hit it face-first and the cold took his breath away. There was nothing but ice and blackness and water. Michael thought, *I'm dying today.*

It seemed an eternity underwater, a lifetime in that place between death and life, but he was not destined to perish that night. Suddenly, his face was out of the water. There was air, so cold it was painful, scorching his starving lungs.

Someone was shouting, "...Grab him, grab him!"

He was hauled up from behind. The dock hit his back, hard. It would hurt when he could feel pain again. Someone else grabbed at his arms, pulling at him, strong but not to the extent of the one who had pulled him up by the jacket.

"Don't let go!" The voice said. He was talking to Michael.

Michael realized that he still held Johnny's arm, caught in a vise-like grip made firmer by the shock of his immersion. How he still held on, he did not know, everything was numb and remote.

Don't let me let go, he prayed. *Don't let me let go...*

He was halfway on the dock now. Linda was saying, "Johnny – save Johnny-"

"I've got him. I've got him, help me."

Someone pulled Johnny's arm away. The hands released Michael. He fell back on the frozen dock and feeling returned with a rush. He rolled over. Linda and the cop were pulling Johnny's limp body out of the water. The cop was on his knees, grunting with effort. Linda pulled at Johnny's arm, slipping on the icy dock. Johnny's head emerged with his face bent in the water. He would drown.

Michael pushed himself to his knees and reached to grab Johnny's shirt.

"Pull!" he ordered.

Linda pulled. The officer expended a massive effort, and the river finally released its victim. Johnny collapsed on top of Michael, bringing them both back down to the dock. Johnny's left arm flung out, his hand smacking against the wood. The knife skittered a few yards away.

Linda immediately bent down to check for vital signs.

"He's alive!" she cried. Her voice was faint against the howl of the wind.

Johnny moaned.

The officer, breathing heavily, stooped over the worn and still bloodied knife and picked it up.

"We've got to get them inside," Linda shouted to him, as though Michael could not hear. "They'll freeze."

The officer nodded. The wind blew his hair wildly and the knife looked small in his hands. He tucked it in his belt and reached down to help Michael to his feet.

"Okay, kids," he said. Even in the wind and the storm, he sounded annoyed. "We'll get you inside and then you all are going to tell your old Uncle Bill what in Hades is going on around here."

CHAPTER 26

The cop was stronger than he looked. He slung Johnny over his shoulder and barreled his way through the snow, back up to the house. Linda followed more slowly, helping Michael. The wind was bitter and the cold was worse. Linda thought that all four of them would need treatment by the time they got inside.

The cop knew where to go. He deposited Johnny in front of the fire and immediately started massaging his legs and arms. Johnny was comatose and white faced. The river had washed some of the blood from his face but not from his shirt.

Michael was shivering. Linda ordered him to get changed, and took over tending to Johnny, stripping off the wet clothes, checking for vital signs again as well as cuts and abrasions with an efficiency that surprised even her.

Michael came back in wrapped in a robe, his wounded arm pressed tight against his chest. He was still shivering but chose to sit on the couch next to his wife rather than by the fire. Linda did not insist. She was too occupied with Johnny.

There was only one cut that she could find, a straight, shallow slash across Johnny's left palm, like a razor cut. It was shallow enough to bleed profusely, but even so...

"Where did all the blood come from?"

The officer's question came from behind Linda, startling her. He was watching her examination, pacing in between her and the couch where Michael sat staring at Susan. He held a bottle of wine and Linda noticed that Michael had a glass too. Alcohol was not the best thing for hypothermia, but it did wonders for the nerves, so she did not object. Rather, she found herself wishing that the policeman would offer her a glass.

Now is not the time for drinking, the scientist in her said. The part of her that was a cowering child replied, *If not now, then when?*

"This is the only wound," she said.

Johnny was breathing evenly now and his color looked good. Despite his immersion into the water and the long cold trudge back to the house, she had been able to stave off frostbite.

Unfortunately, that was not the only thing that they had to worry about.

"That wouldn't account for all the blood we saw," the officer pointed out.

He kept his voice low as if wary of disturbing Susan...or was it that he did not want Michael to hear? Linda noticed the look he kept shooting at Michael, a suspicious, wary look. Why this was, she did not know, and where *had* Susan got those cuts on her face?

"I know," she said and finished wrapping the wound. "But there are no other cuts."

"Is there anyone else in the house?" he asked.

Linda bit her lip.

The officer crouched down beside her. His eyes were steady and his mouth was set in a firm line.

"Come on, kid," he said. "It's better if you're straight with me."

She looked at him and thought, *He's the only sane one here right now.*

"You'd better sit down," she recommended.

He did, and she told him everything.

***

It was only after she was finished that it occurred to Linda that she didn't know who she was talking to. Fortunately, the officer seemed much more eager to answer questions than address the current crisis.

His name was Bill Emery and he was up from Boston visiting relatives, most of whom were also local cops and volunteer firemen. Technically, he was on vacation but volunteered to help when the surprise storm hit. He ended up on the Reynolds road by accident; a series of fallen trees, snow drifts, and ice slicks had seen to that. He had not intended on stopping but when he saw Michael's flag and the crumpled sedan under the snow he had decided that he had better check it out.

"I thought I was just here to help out with blankets and necessities." His gaze kept darting from Linda to Michael, who still sat motionless on the couch watching Susan. "I didn't know I'd be walking into something like this."

"Like what?" Linda asked.

Emery hesitated and looked over towards the couch. Then he leaned over and said, in a tone low enough so that Michael couldn't hear.

"Be frank with me, okay? He hits her, right?"

"*What?*" Linda glared at him. "Are you crazy?"

"After what happened in that ballroom, I'm not so sure anymore," Emery muttered. "But if he isn't hitting her, can you explain what happened to her face?"

Linda looked over at the couch. Susan was curled up under the blanket, her face turned away from the fire. Linda had been so busy with Johnny she hadn't thought to check Susan, assuming, when she saw her friend on the couch, that she hadn't woken. But *why* wasn't she awake? Surely there had been enough noise to…

Alarmed, Linda jumped up and went over to the couch, moving Michael aside so that she could examine Susan.

Emery was right. Something had done a number on Susan's face. Dried blood crusted around the shallow cut marks and the very sight of them made Linda feel angry and protective. Otherwise, Susan seemed unhurt, just pale and in an unusually heavy sleep.

Linda turned on Michael. "What happened to her, Michael?" When Michael looked hesitantly at Emery, she snapped, "*He* thinks you hit her."

"I never-" he protested and Emery said, "Look, isolation like this can…"

Linda cut them both off. "What *happened*, Michael?

His explanation satisfied no one.

"Come on." Emery stepped forward, glowering at Michael. "Do you really expect me to believe haunted *books* attacked your wife?"

Michael looked haggard.

"I don't expect you to believe anything," he said. "I don't know what to believe myself."

145

He glanced at his wife and Linda thought, with a pang, *He still doesn't know about the child.*

Emery was not happy. He ran a hand through his hair and was about to say something when there came a loud banging from upstairs. He stopped cold and his eyes met Linda's.

"A shutter," she said simply. "That's all."

He seemed disgusted, more at himself than anything else. "Naturally," he said and looked at the bottle of wine as though he wished it were whiskey. "Naturally."

There was silence for a moment.

Linda looked at her brother's wounded hand, his *left* hand. She thought about how he had waved it about in the ballroom, the curious lilt in his voice when he had asked '*Why?*' and the way his right arm had dangled uselessly throughout, as though forgotten. She remembered his reaction when she called him '*Charlie*'. She didn't know why she'd said that. It seemed the most natural thing in the world to do, although she had not forgotten for a second that he was Johnny...or at least that the body was Johnny's. The spirit ...well, that was something else altogether.

Johnny was lying peacefully now. Among the things in her emergency kit were a few doses of sedatives, something which she used herself from time to time. They were easily dissolved in a few drops of wine, which Johnny had taken quietly. He would sleep and sleep would protect him.

She hoped it would, anyway.

Linda had realized two very uncomfortable things. One was that while Susan and Johnny had acted as though possessed by something, no one else had mentioned seeing or hearing anything. Linda had heard the music. She heard the children in the hall. She had almost seen the dancers in the ballroom. The only exception to this was that both Michael and Bill Emery had acted as though they had noticed the presence of others in the ballroom once Johnny had entered. That meant that she was not crazy, small comfort there.

The other realization was much more spine chilling. Susan had awakened terrified in Rachel's room. Later, she had been attacked in the den. Twice now, Johnny had tried to throw himself off the dock and into the river. Linda was seeing things. But someone seemed to be actively trying to kill Johnny and Susan.

She said aloud, "Johnny was Charles Reynolds in there. You know that, of course."

Michael stirred, but it was Emery who spoke.

"The guy who died twenty-five years ago?" He snorted. "Come on."

"He didn't use his right hand and there were all those... those people." She pinned Emery with a look. "You felt them too."

Bill Emery had the grace to appear uncomfortable. "Come on, lady," he said. "All sorts of things go on in your head when you've been using."

"Johnny *hasn't* been using!" she spat. "And neither have I! Check his arms if you don't believe me. Look at his eyes. He's *clean* and so were you."

"Linda." Michael was gentle. "What are you saying happened in there?"

She did not want to say it. She did not want to believe it. But the truth was pressing on her and the pressure was more than she could take. If she was going off the deep end, so be it. It *had* to be said.

"We aren't alone in this house," she said. "Charles Reynolds didn't kill his wife. He's been trying to tell us that all evening. We just haven't wanted to listen."

CHAPTER 27

Bill Emery thought, *And I thought you were the sane one, lady.*

He shouldn't have been surprised. After all, the first time he laid eyes on her the woman had been dancing in the middle of that ballroom with an invisible being. But she had come to so swiftly and so sensibly; checking vital signs, helped the wife-beater into the house, and taking care of the wounded with a professional detachment that frankly impressed him. She was a solid person, this Linda Vincent. Pretty too, with that cinnamon-colored hair and those deep brown eyes. Not that he was the type to be swayed by a pretty face…

At least, he had *thought* she was sensible and solid. Now here she was, demanding that he, William G. Emery, a realist to the core, believe in spirits of the dead.

Ridiculous, he thought.

But then again, he *had* been there in the ballroom. He had felt the presence of others, had been jostled by invisible hands, and what was worse, he had heard the cries of dismay when the nut-job took off for the door.

Imagination, he thought, but he was not the imaginative type any more than Linda was hysterical.

Figures. Here I was, coming home for a home-cooked meal and a relaxing, boring Christmas with the folks. Instead, I end up in a mad house full of lunatics who think it's Halloween.

If he could have left River House right there and then, he would have. He'd have slapped the cuffs on Michael Wright and left Linda with the battered wife while he radioed in the situation. But he couldn't. His radio had gone dead ten minutes before he'd set eyes on River House, and his car had stalled in the driveway. When he had tried to restart it, the engine wouldn't even turn over – the battery was as dead as Dickens' coffin nail.

Emery was stranded here in a house full of nut-jobs and a pretty, sensible woman who was rapidly, tragically going mad.

Typical, he thought. *Goes to show you never can win.*

He and Michael Wright sat by the fire, waiting for Linda, who was sorting through a stack of papers and magazines on the table. The fire held off the darkness and the shadows did not seem to press in as they once had. Michael looked strung-out and beaten. His encounter in the den had shaken him to the core and he rubbed his arm obsessively. When Bill asked about it, Michael merely shrugged.

"I hurt it in the accident," he said. "Wrestling with Johnny made it worse."

"Is it broken?"

Michael shook his head. "I don't know. It's next to useless now."

Bill thought, *Won't be able to hit your wife for a little bit anyway,* but his heart wasn't really in it. He was no longer sure of his assessment of the situation.

Linda came over and to the fireplace and lowered herself beside Bill. She handed him a handwritten page, then stretched across him to hand a similar page to Michael. Bill caught a whiff of rose-scented soap as she came close. He was relieved when she settled back into her place.

"Mr. Emery, you're a detective," she said, looking up at him with big brown eyes like rich caramel. "Maybe you can help us figure this out."

When he looked down, he saw a timeline which had been written out by a shaky hand. It was Rachel Reynolds' old research. Emery's Uncle George, who had been sheriff off and on in the town for about twenty years, used to talk about Rachel's time-lines. Only the other day, when talking about the River House article in the Triple Town Sentry, he'd told Bill that the one thing he did not miss about being retired was the annual letter from Rachel Reynolds demanding that the case be reopened.

"Rich old nut-bird," was Uncle George's opinion. "Convinced that someone was trying to poison her nephew and that's why he went off his rocker. He was crazy long before pills were involved."

As he was considered the expert on the Reynolds affair, Bill hadn't questioned his assessment.

"Look, lady, this case was closed years ago," Bill said. "What is there to figure out?"

She rubbed her arms against a sudden chill. "According to the report, Charles Reynolds was angry with his wife so he overdosed himself with his medication, went up to her room, slashed her throat, then came back downstairs to throw himself off the dock."

"Right. This time-line bears it out."

"It seems to. But my brother brought up a good point a little while back. Charles had already overdosed himself *and* he had a razor in his hand. Why did he run out to the dock to drown himself?"

"It does seem like overkill," Michael said, then flushed. "Sorry."

Emery shrugged. "Okay, it's a little weird," he admitted. "But the guy was all drugged up and he wasn't in his right mind to begin with. That's why he was committing suicide."

"But it couldn't have been Charles." Linda leaned forward, her eyes glittering in excitement. "I told you about Susan's dream earlier, when she was reliving Helene's experience."

Bill shifted uncomfortably, thinking, *Oh, geez, lady…*

She took no notice of his discomfort. "In her dream, a man came in and put one hand on her mouth and held the razor in the *other*!"

She looked at him in bright expectancy and he almost hated himself for asking, "So?"

"So it couldn't have been Charles she saw. He lost his *right* hand in the war. He only had the one hand to use! You see, it *had* to be someone else."

"Yeah, but, look… it only was a dream, kid."

"It wasn't just a dream," Linda insisted. "She was reliving the experience."

"*Or* she was just dreaming. You guys were all talking about the case before she came up here, right? She went to bed with murder on her mind and had a nightmare. That's not proof, Linda. It's not evidence. It's not even real. It's just one woman's very active imagination."

"If you knew Susan," Michael said, "you would not dismiss it so easily."

The comment surprised Bill. He looked from Linda to Michael and saw the same fanatical gleam in their eyes. They *really* believed that this Helene ghost had come and shown the battered wife a vision.

I'm stuck in a houseful of loonies, he thought. His momentary fear turned into annoyance, but when he turned to Linda to read her the riot act, she spoke first.

"You saw what happened in the ballroom," she said quietly. "You heard them, you saw them, *and* you saw the blood on Johnny's shirt and hands. Remembering that, can you *really* tell me that there are no ghosts in this house?"

Under normal circumstances, Bill would have been out of there, chalking up the craziness to pot or whatever it was the kids were smoking these days. He would have chided Linda for wasting his time, for giving in to the atmosphere of isolation and superstition, for making a fool of herself and him. But the woman who was looking at him had grit and determination and she didn't look like anyone's fool.

What was worse, she was right. He had been in that ballroom when things got... well, weird, and he couldn't explain it. Not in a way that would make him happy, anyway.

He looked over at the husband. Michael was sitting still, watching him with a weariness that spoke of acceptance. He wasn't hysterical and his eyes were clear. He didn't look like a user, but they didn't always.

"You're both crazy," he said, because dealing with crazy was better than what they were asking him to believe.

Michael shrugged. "If we are, you are, too."

Bill looked at Linda. She was watching him levelly, measuring his response, and there was not a trace of hysteria about her.

You're stuck here anyway, Bill. Might as well go along with it until you can figure out what's really going on.

"All right, sister, you win," he said. "Since there doesn't seem to be anything else to do tonight, you want to lay more of that theory on me?"

CHAPTER 28

Linda didn't care that Bill Emery was just humoring her. He was listening and that was enough. She would make her case and if she could convince Emery, a stranger, a lawman and a detective, that not only did ghosts exist, but they were present and active in River House, then it was so and she wasn't crazy. If she couldn't convince him... But that was a problem she could deal with later.

The wind howled about the eaves of the house. The building settled creakingly into place, its groans and grimaces hardly noticeable above the sound of the storm outside. It was not roaring as loud as it had been earlier, but it would be a mistake to think that the blizzard was over. It was far from finished. This was the lull in battle when the soldiers regroup and take stock for the final, fatal thrust.

At least, that was how Linda thought of it. She knew little of the spirit world, however she did know that spirits were not all powerful, merely persistent. For the moment, house was quiet and the living had time to themselves but this peace would not last long. Until Charles's mission was complete, the hauntings would continue.

Despite his disbelief, she was glad that she was sitting at Emery's side. Emery exuded confidence and competence and the fact that he was an armed police office was also reassuring. Useless as the gun might be, Linda felt better that it was there.

Michael said, "If we assume that Charles is not the killer, who is left?"

"The one who gained the most from his death," Emery said promptly. "Always look to the money."

"Which, in this case, would mean Jacob North," Linda said.

"He was in the study when Charles was killing his wife," Michael said. "Besides, Charles himself took the pills, didn't he? Doesn't that indicate suicide?"

Linda looked into the fire, thinking about prescription pills and visiting nurses and the stories older nurses used to tell during late night shifts at the hospital. One nurse in particular had been assigned to a household with a man suffering from nightmares like Charles had.

She said aloud, "If Charles really was suffering from mood swings, they wouldn't have allowed him unfettered access to his medications. His nurse would keep the pills herself and only give him what was prescribed for that dose."

"Meaning he'd have to hoard the medication in order to overdose," Emery said.

"Meaning suicide," Michael said.

"Meaning *premeditated* suicide," Emery corrected. "That's a whole different ballgame. Who was his assigned nurse?"

"Irene Simmons North, the woman who married the heir," Linda said.

"When Charles died, his grandfather's ward, my boss, took over the company," Michael explained to Emery.

"That's a helluva good motive," Emery said. "Kill the soldier-boy and take over the megabucks."

"But Jacob was in the den at the time of the killing," Michael pointed out. "There's no access to Helene's room

154

except by the front staircase and there were witnesses that say he never came up. Besides, he wouldn't have access to the medication, nor would he be able to slip Charles the pills. He'd only just come home to a house full of guests."

"But Irene could," Linda said, "And don't forget, she was engaged to Jacob at the time. Rachel said that Helene was convinced that someone was messing with Charles' medications and that stuff he was on..." She broke off, shuddering.

Emery was watching her thoughtfully. "Pretty powerful, huh?"

She nodded. "Mood altering and dangerous if you start to muck around."

"But doesn't that tend to prove that Charles did murder Helene?" Michael asked. "If he was starting to lose it and let's say that Irene was messing about with his doses - even granting that she was trying to kill him, for which we have no proof - that would only strengthen the murder case. Charles — or someone else - was messing with the dosages of his mood-altering medications, which heightened his sense of being wronged, so he lashed out at his wife. He may not have been morally at fault, but he *must* have killed her."

"No, no, it's all wrong, Michael," Linda cried out. "He wouldn't have killed his wife. Everyone said so. Rachel ruined her life trying to prove it. There must be another explanation. There has to be. Jacob..."

"Jacob was in the den, then he went outside," Emery said. "Why?"

Michael looked startled. "Why?"

"Why?" Emery repeated. "The party was inside. Linda said he'd only just come up from Boston. He took a phone call, then he went outside, on a frigid night, and apparently just wandered around until he saw the nut job trying to kill himself. But why did *he* go outside?"

Michael was flummoxed. Linda was looking thoughtful.

"You know..." she said, "Helene was trying to surprise Charles with the baby and Irene was looking after both of them. It's very likely that she would have known about the baby, or at least figured it out."

"With a baby Reynolds on the way, Grandpa wouldn't have given the business to North." Emery said. "That gives North and his little tootsie a very good reason to kill Helene as well, especially if Helene was already suspicious of Irene and the dosages. If she'd lived and carried the baby to term, killing Charles would have been for nothing."

Michael said sharply, "But even if she did suspect that Helene was pregnant, that doesn't change anything! Helene was alive when Irene and the maid went to see her and she was alive when they left. There's only one door to Helene's room and according to witnesses, only one person went in after them. Charles *had* to have killed Helene. He was the only one who went into that room and he-"

He broke off. The house had come alive. The wind had risen once again, crashing against the side of the house, making the shutters jump and rattle all up and down the building. The fire roared to life and Johnny, lying on his back, began to moan and squirm. From up above, a door slammed and the chandelier in the entryway rattled violently until it sounded as though it were going to come down.

Emery jumped to his feet and raced to the entryway with Linda fast on his heels. A cold blast of air greeted them at the doorway, whipping Linda's hair and screaming in her ear. The chandelier swayed and bucked and then, without warning, the little table in the entryway flipped over and smashed into the wall just inches from where Emery stood watching. Linda screamed and pressed her hand to her mouth.

But it was all over. The temper tantrum had passed with minimal damage to the hall. There was a whisper like someone moving away and then the room was still.

Emery put a reassuring hand on her shoulder and turned to Michael. "Someone didn't like your reasoning there."

Michael stood in the middle of the living room, a thin, wasted figure in the darkness. For the first time since Linda had met him, he looked really frightened.

"You were right, Linda," he whispered. "We aren't here by accident." He swallowed hard, looking at his wife. "We're stuck here, in this house...and it's all my fault..."

"Stop it." Emery took a step forward, pointing a finger at him. "We haven't the time for another meltdown." He turned to Linda. "I don't know what that *was* in the hallway out there, but let's say you're right; something brought us all here, destroying your car and killing mine. If that's true, they're not going to let us leave here without a fight, right?"

"Right," Linda said, her voice cracking.

"And there's no way we can leave here tonight, not with this storm." Emery said. "We're trapped until we figure this thing out. So we'd better do it." He folded his arms. "So where do we start?"

Linda felt her heart sink. She thought of the steep staircase, the dreadfully long, dim hallway and the sounds of the children's laughter. She thought of Susan stretched out and white as a corpse on Helene's old bed, then sitting up, terror-crazed, to speak to Michael in French. Susan did not speak French... but Helene did.

Linda thought of the music box and that darkness...that terrible, thick, cloying darkness that seeped into your bones until you became one with it.

She knew where they had to start, but it was the last place on earth that she wanted to go.

Emery was watching her. Michael was too. Beyond them she saw Johnny with his bloodstained shirt and drawn face, looking as though he had aged a decade since the afternoon. For good or evil, something had used him and if she did nothing, they might not be able to save Johnny the next time the ghost came to call. She had to act, for his sake and for Susan's.

So many times had Susan taken the lead on things, so many times had Linda surrendered to her good sense and strong will. Now it was Linda's turn to take the lead. It was a terrifying prospect.

She had to go back up there, into the dark, into the memory of that night twenty-five years ago. She had to confront the ghosts of the past. There was no other way.

She had not realized that she had been reaching into her pocket when her hands found her rosary beads. She gripped it like a lifeline, so tightly that the metal chain bit into her hand.

For Johnny and Susan, then.

"If I'm right about Jacob, there's another way into Helene's room," she said. "We start in there."

CHAPTER 29

Emery was not the type of man who wasted time on feelings and emotions. He did not like what he called 'big productions' or grandstanding. If you decided on a course of action, you should follow it with minimum time, waste, and fuss.

Linda wanted to go upstairs into the dead woman's room. It seemed like a good idea from an investigatory standpoint. It was the scene of the crime after all. Watching her talk about it with that guy, Michael (whom Emery still eyed with suspicion), you would have thought there was still an active crime taking place, not a preserved site from twenty-five years ago. Sure, Linda had mentioned the children in the hallway, her brother's odd behavior when he entered the room, and Michael told them of his wife's bizarre speech when she awoke from her nightmare, but they were clearly easily suggestable people.

Emery was not. 'Hard-headed' was the phrase people most often used when trying to describe him and he readily confessed to the charge. But what most people forgot or did not know was that there was a noble streak that ran about a foot wide down Emery's back. He would never admit to *that* of course, but it was that noble streak that kept his mouth shut when Linda was rambling in the living room and it was that streak that had him following her up the staircase towards a dead woman's bedroom.

Linda led the way, holding a candle in one hand and keeping her other hand firmly in her pocket. The house creaked and groaned around them, but there was no repeat of the little performance in the hall earlier.

Emery found himself saying, "If there was ever a place that could convince me of hauntings this would be it."

Linda turned, her eyebrows knitted in puzzlement. "You *still* don't believe?"

"Let's just say the jury is still out."

She seemed about to say something, thought the better of it, and started up again.

Emery glanced back to the doorway of the living room. Michael was inside, keeping an eye on the patients and nursing his arm. Emery had not really liked the idea of leaving the man alone with his wife but he had liked the idea of him going alone with Linda even less. To his surprise, Linda, too, insisted that Emery, not Michael, accompany her to Helene's room.

They were at the top of the stairs now. Linda stopped, looking into the inky blackness of the hall with some trepidation. Emery did not blame her. Even without all the weirdness going on, it was downright spooky.

He turned on the flashlight and shone the beam around the hall.

"Nothing," he said and smiled when she looked at him. "No spooks."

She nodded but did not smile back. "It was brave of you to come," she said. "You know, considering... everything."

She sounded really frightened.

"Oh," Emery tried to shrug it off. "The dead aren't anything to be scared of. It is the living that can kill you. Besides, I haven't been spooked since I was a kid, watching Boris Karloff."

"I've never seen his movies."

To his left, a breeze caught the chandelier, making the crystals jingle. Emery only just stopped himself from jumping.

"He could have learned something from this place," he admitted.

Now she did smile.

They started down the hall and Emery asked, "So… why me, huh?" When she looked at him in puzzlement, he explained, "Why not Michael? I figured from the way you told him to stay behind that, well, you had a theory about something."

"He's related," she said. She walked stiffly, as though expecting to be approached at any minute. "His mother is a Reynolds, distant cousins or something. I thought if the ghosts were going to take anyone else, he'd be next."

"You think there's more than one ghost?"

"Oh, yes." She glanced up at him. "Don't you?"

When he didn't answer, she went on. "They… got to Johnny and Susan. They tried me, too, but it didn't take."

"Why your brother? He's not related."

"He's already dealing with his own demons. I guess his defenses were down."

"Vietnam?"

She looked surprised. "How did you know?"

Emery shrugged. "He had the look."

They were standing at the end of the hall and there was a door on either side of them. It was cooler down here but not enough to cause concern. Linda reached for one of the handles, hesitated, then wrenched the door open.

The room smelled of cinnamon and cloves and it was dark as pitch, even with the two light sources. Emery stood just inside the doorway, watching Linda as she hesitantly moved about the bed. He felt his own nerves fraying. It was outwardly quiet and peaceful but there was a feeling in this room, a feeling of being watched.

"So, uh," he said, trying to make some noise to cover his own growing sense of unease. "What are you looking for?"

Linda stood at the foot of the bed looking at the pile of neglected blankets. The flickering light of the candle cast weird shadows on her face.

"I don't know," she said. She traced the outline of mattress with her hand. "I wonder what Helene was trying to tell Susan by reliving what happened?"

He didn't say anything.

She sighed and shook her head at him. "You still don't believe."

"I believe in facts."

"Just the facts, ma'am," she said in a gently mocking tone. She walked around to the other side of the bed. "There has to be another way into this room."

"If there was, wouldn't the old broad who lived here…"

"Rachel."

"Wouldn't Rachel know about it?" he asked.

She hesitated. "Probably, but it's the only explanation that makes sense. If it wasn't Charles, then it had to be someone else and that person needed a way in here…"

"If it was someone else," Emery muttered.

The door to the bedroom burst open and a whirl of cold air rushed through, whipping past him. He jumped and swore. Linda squealed and ran over to his side. The wind stopped almost as soon as it came. They stood close together, the two strangers, and Emery became aware of two things: the tight clench of Linda's arms around his left arm and the feeling that the temperature had just dropped by ten degrees.

"Just the wind," he said gruffly.

"You don't hear them?" Her breathing was heavy.

"Hear what?"

"The children."

Emery felt as though all the strength was leaching out of his legs. "The *what?*"

Linda's grip tightened. Her eyes were focused on the far side of the room. "They're by the closet."

He turned his flashlight to scan the area, but there was nothing to see. No one was there.

She let go of his arm and stepped forward. "What are they looking at?"

"Oh, come on, kid!" Emery's heart pounded in his chest. He was trying his best not to panic but if she was going to go off the deep end like that... "Quit trying to scare an old man, will you?"

She was in front of the closet now and reaching for the doors.

"Wait!" Emery said. He was not fast enough. She threw them open.

Nothing happened. No one jumped out. No one reached for her. It was just a closet filled with women's clothes and heavy with the scent of moth balls and dust.

He sneezed and felt disgusted. Linda was laughing at him.

"Come on," he muttered and moved to get away from the dust.

"I'm sorry," she said. "It's just that I suddenly got the feeling that... I don't know, that everything was going to be all right somehow. Here, let's switch, shall we?" She held out the candle and he reluctantly exchanged it for the flashlight.

"Besides," she said, turning back to the closet, "you aren't old. What are you, forty? Forty-five?"

"None of your business," he said, without rancor. "Too old for this nonsense, that's for sure."

"Oh, you just have no spirit of adventure." She leaned into the closet, pressing on the back wall.

"I wish you wouldn't use the word spirit," he groaned then scowled. "What's gotten into you? Weren't you the one that was terrified a minute ago?"

"Yes," her voice was muffled by the clothes. "I was. I should still be I guess, it's just… well, like I said, I suddenly got the feeling that we're all going to be all right – oh, what's this?"

"What's what?" Emery asked and then jumped again. Something had moved only a few feet away from him, just out of his range of sight. Someone was there, someone who was breathing very, very gently.

He reached for his gun as Linda answered, "I don't know – a loose panel I think. I'm going to push it."

"You do that." Emery said, forcing his voice to stay level.

His gun was in his hand. The person, whoever it was, was standing in the corner by the bed, just beyond the reach of his candle. He could almost make out a shape now out of the corner of his eye. It was an inch shorter than he and it was waiting for something.

Human, he thought. He ought to have been relieved. He was not. He hadn't been kidding when he told Linda that he feared the living far more than the dead.

Linda, unaware of the intruder, grunted to herself in the closet. The intruder had not moved. He or she apparently did not know that Emery had seen it, for it stood there, watching and waiting. Emery could almost feel the anxiety emanating from the intruder.

He or she was upset. They would act and when they did, they would act rashly...which meant Emery had to make the first move.

"I almost have it..." Linda was saying, frustrated.

"That's great, honey." Emery said, shifting his feet. "That's great..."

That was when the music box started playing, erupting with sound from the table at Emery's side.

Emery jumped, turning as he did, gun out and candle thrust forward against the gloom. His eyes caught movement and went to the table first, where a tiny ghostly pair twirled about to the song. Then he looked at the corner.

All he got was a glance...a woman stood there, transfixed in horror, anger, and rage, her hands clutching her robes. She was wiry and her gray hair was loose on her shoulders. The look she threw Emery was pure venom. Her mouth twisted into a snarl. Her hand released its hold on her skirt so as to reach out for him...

"Got it!" Linda shouted.

Emery blinked.

The woman dove right for Emery...and vanished.

Emery staggered, overcome with a rushing sensation as though he had just gone on an acid trip. An acid trip in Antarctica, for the freezing cold that came with it was enough to make him lose his breath. He lost his grip on the gun, lost the strength in his legs. As he came crashing down to the floor he heard two things: the music box plaintively singing '*I'll be Home for Christmas*' and Linda's terrified shriek...

CHAPTER 30

Michael was pacing in front of the fireplace when he heard it…a sharp intake of breath, like the gasp of a small child.

He started and at once looked to Johnny who was stretched out on the floor very near him. The soldier's breathing was shallow and his pallor had not improved even with the drug induced sleep. A few minutes ago he had begun to toss and turn and mutter. Michael tried not to listen. He was focused on the couple upstairs, listening for cries for help or…or whatever. He could not keep from hearing snatches of what Johnny was saying.

"Keep your head down. *Down*, damn you!…Orders just came in…"

Johnny was reliving the war, but that was not unusual. What was strange was that at times he seemed to be reliving a war he had not been in. German names mixed in with Asian. Once he sobbed briefly, "My hand… my hand…"

It was unnerving and Michael did not like it. He stood by Johnny's side as the ex-soldier writhed, wondering if he ought to wake him up. Linda had given Johnny sedatives and surely they would kick in.

They must have, for now the mutterings had stopped and Johnny was lying quietly. It was Susan that had gasped.

She was sitting bolt upright, alert and nervous, looking up at the ceiling, so still that at first Michael did not notice that she had moved. When he did, he sprinted to her side.

"Susan? Honey?"

She did not look at him. She did not even hear him. She remained where she was, eyes focused on the ceiling, tension radiating from her body. Now that he was close he could see that her eyes were glazed over. She was not awake. She was still sleeping…or worse.

He touched her shoulder gently and she gasped.

"Elle est *la*!" she said in a hoarse whisper. "Elle est revenue. Elle est *revenue*…"

It was not Susan's voice. It was a hollow sound, a distant, deathly sound and she hissed around the words. Michael took her shoulder and turned her.

"Susan, honey, wake up."

"Elle est la," she said more loudly. "Elle est revenue." Then she looked at him. The expression on her face was hard and angry. "Ou est votre manteau, frere?" she asked and Michael's blood went cold at the mocking tone. "Ou est-ce?"

She began to chant the words over and over again, rocking her body in time to their rhythm. "Ou est votre manteau, eh? Ou est-ce? Ou est-ce?"

"Susan, wake up," Michael ordered. His own voice was growing shrill with panic. He shook her hard. "Susan, wake *up*!"

But she did not. She just kept rocking and crying out in French. Michael would not leave her, could not take his eyes off of her face. He was so occupied that he did not even notice when Johnny left the room.

CHAPTER 31

One minute, Linda was in the closet playing with the panel, feeling, for the first time since she had arrived at River House that she was in control and on top of things. In the next, the wall had disappeared. She was falling and the flashlight had gone out. She hit cold wooden planks and dust flew up and choked her. She sneezed and coughed several times, the contraction of muscles reviving the dull aches and pains from the car accident earlier in the day.

There was a sliding sound, and wood screamed as it was wrenched out of place. Then came the curious sensation of cold crawling *over* her back. She wriggled and squeaked at the feeling.

Then there was silence.

She lay there for a moment, trying to recover herself. It had been cold enough in Helene's room, but it was positively frigid in here – wherever *here* was. The wind was louder too as the storm battered away at the siding. When she shifted, she felt cool air pouring over her neck and she thought, *It was just a draft, that's all. It's an old house.*

She propped herself up on one arm and reached out with the other, hoping to find the flashlight. She traced her hand through decades of dust and cobwebs before her fingertip found the smooth, round surface.

Thank God!

She snapped it on just as Emery began pounding on the door.

"Linda? Linda, are you all right?"

His anxiety poured through the paneling, warming her.

"I'm fine!" she said. "Just a little...shaken..."

Her voice echoed in the small space. She shone the light around and found that she was on a landing. Unfinished crossbeams, hung thickly with cobwebbing, crisscrossed the walls on either side of her. A narrow staircase descended, winding down into the darkness, barely wide enough for her slender frame. It was only inches from where she sat. If she had rolled the wrong way to get up, she would have lost her balance and fallen down, like Irene had on the staircase.

At the thought of Irene's death, her heart began to pound.

Why were you up that night? Did you hear the children, too? Did you know about these stairs?

Emery's voice broke through her silent inquiry, "Hang on a second, I'll get you out of there."

"Bill! I've found it!" She felt about for a door handle or latch. There was nothing, only solid board through which not a particle of light fell. She kept searching, talking all the while, "There's a staircase here, leading downstairs, Bill! They must have known about it, Charles, Jacob, and Irene. They were kids growing up here. Maybe that's who I heard in the hallway... they were trying to show me the way here."

There came only muttered swears from the other side.

"Did you hear me, Bill? There's a staircase!"

"Yeah, yeah, I heard it. I'm trying to open this door..."

"Jacob must have used this staircase that night," she said. "They must have kept it a secret from Rachel and that night, when he was supposed to be on the phone..."

"Does it go into the den?"

Leave it to Bill Emery to come up with the practical question. She wondered if he was as pragmatic on the job as he was here.

Still, he was right. If the staircase curved down into, say, the ballroom or the basement, her theory was blown and the case remained open. There was only one thing to do.

She called through the paneling, "I don't know, but I'll go see."

"No, wait a minute…"

She was already making her way down the stairs.

The open, unfinished walls on either side of the stairs made sort of cubby holes where the wooden bracing lay exposed. She could hear the storm more clearly here, roaring like a wild thing outside. There was some snow, too, leaking through the places where time had warped the siding. The steps creaked ominously as she stepped on them.

The house is old — the wood could be rotting…

Even as she thought this the step gave with a sharp crack. Her foot fell through rotten wood, scraping painfully on shards and twisting. She cried out and managed to catch herself on one of the cubby holes. Her hand slipped on cloth, then caught hold of solid beam while her foot came to rest on something under the stairs.

Linda gasped for breath, shaken. Her arm was sore from the shock of the fall but she had managed to keep hold of the flashlight.

She heard pounding coming from upstairs.

She shouted, "I'm all right, I'm all right!" and stopped short when she heard a new sound.

It was like a whisper, soft, indistinct, and only a few steps down from her. Her breath caught. She whipped the flashlight around, but of course, there was nothing.

Probably just the children again. They want me to keep going. No reason to be frightened. They're just here to help.

She pushed herself off of the wall and in doing so touched the cloth again. She brought the beam around and found herself looking at a handful of brown, dusty, satin fabric. There were mounds of it. When Linda picked it up, she realized that she was holding a man's long great coat, turned inside out.

Susan's words came back to her, *"Ou est tu manteau?"*

With shaking fingers she turned the coat right side out while holding the flashlight under her arm. It was a fine old coat, made of good material and masterfully cut. Neglect and time wore its grandeur and it was crusted with caked-on dust and mold. There were great splashes of stains running down the front, causing the fabric to stick together in places. When she turned the flashlight onto the stains, she saw that they were black and stiff, like dried blood.

Her heart was pounding in her throat. She was so absorbed in her discovery, so intent on finding a label that she did not notice the temperature sliding down or the unnatural silence that grew and centered near her. She was close to the answer and that was all Linda could see, feel, or hear.

At last she located the label. It had been custom made and the tailor had seen fit to put both his name and the name of the coat's owner on the collar. She angled the flashlight until she could see the names, *"Felix Tailoring – Mr. Jacob R. North."*

I was right. Here is the proof…

The scream that cut her off was not her own. She fell back against the wall, the coat falling from her fingers, the flashlight too, but she had no more need of light. The stairway was suddenly flooded with it, brought by the same person who stood before her, wavering and terrible.

Then it was as if all the darkness in the house converged upon that one spot where Linda stood. She cried out but it did no good. She was falling, falling, where no one could reach her. There was only the shadows, the cold, and the evil that remained.

CHAPTER 32

Charles was present.

His arrival was swift and overwhelming and his need was so great that for a few moments Johnny lost track of where Charles ended and Johnny began. He wrestled with the man at first, tossing back and forth as they fought for mastery of the body. Johnny was terrified and with good reason. Charles had already tried to kill him twice. He'd brought Johnny to his knees in darkness and terror, then threatened Linda with Johnny's own knife. Johnny would rather have drowned in the river than allowed the man access again.

Johnny had known Charles would return, that he would wait until Johnny was weak to try again. Johnny was exhausted. His defenses were even lower than they had been before. He'd hoped that the drugs Linda had given him would render his body useless even to specters, but it appeared that Charles wasn't to be put off. When he came, it was a full on assault.

Still, Johnny fought. He would not be used as a tool to hurt others, especially not Linda, not his sister. Death was better. The abyss was better.

In the end, Charles won. He forced Johnny up onto his feet and guided his steps forward. It was Charles who saw what Michael could not see; that Helene was trying to shield and protect the shell, the woman called Susan. Because Charles saw this, Johnny did too and stopped fighting so hard. There was more going on here than mere possession.

They were walking into the den now. The evil had fled, leaving only moldy traces behind. The books lay scattered on the floor where she had flung them. Charles saw them and said, *It was not Othello but Macbeth.*

Whatever that meant.

Charles did not speak, not really. It was not necessary as long as they both stayed in the same shell. This ease of communication also meant that keeping Johnny's identity separate was a struggle. To his surprise, he found that Charles, also, was trying to keep his identity his own.

There is an evil you must face, Charles told him.

I cannot, Johnny said. *I am too weak.*

You must.

They stopped in front of the back wall of the den where an empty, shallow bookcase stood. Charles guided his hand to the shelf, to the lever. It was stiff with time, for no one had touched it since that day, twenty-five years ago.

Rachel Reynolds had kept everyone out, protecting their secret without realizing what she was doing. Irene had returned ten years ago to protect another secret, and in doing so she had been frightened into falling down the stairs. Not Charles' doing, nor Helene's. All it took to kill Irene was a guilty conscious.

The shelf pulled away from the wall and Johnny was flooded with memories. He was a small boy, gasping at the discovery. Jacob was there, weird, awkward little Jacob with the shadowy eyes. He had been Charles' friend by necessity and the secret of the stairs had been theirs alone.

Until Irene found out.

He saw her as a child again, thin-faced and always looking hungry. She was well fed – no one who worked for Grandfather suffered monetarily – but Irene had a chronic condition; she could never be satisfied.

Other memories fell hard after that; the war, the draft, the look on Irene's face when he rejected her at that last dance before he left for the base.

"You're like my sister, Irene…I could never think of you that way…"

Then there was the explosion, the pain, waking up in that prisoner-of-war camp, Sergeant Koepple, then his release…and Helene. The memories came like flashcards, flipping faster and faster. Then they slowed almost to a halt. He was home again, in his house. Helene was there, sitting on the bed with him, her honey blonde hair spilling down her back while an expression of concern creased her beautiful face.

"This isn't natural, Charlie. The medicine shouldn't be affecting you this way. There is something wrong…"

She meant Irene.

Then the scene changed. It was the party. He was staggering up the stairs. He had not believed Helene, not really, but nevertheless, he had not taken the medication that Irene had given him that night. He had slipped it into his pocket instead. But he was still staggering and he did not know why. He had had one drink, just one…but it was one that Irene had poured.

She's slipped something in it…

He went to the bedroom. He wanted to see Helene, to ask her for help because he was frightened. He reached for the handle. He opened the door. Helene was stretched out on the bed, asleep, looking like an angel in white lace. There was danger in this room. They couldn't stay – she couldn't be allowed to sleep. He reached for her, but then the floor rushed up to meet him as the drugs took their full effect…

Charles shuddered then, as though drawing a steadying breath.

It hurts, he said to Johnny. *You understand. The memories can be more painful than the actualities. But you must see. You must understand.*

They were on the floor of Helene's room. The doctored drink that Irene had given Charles was meant to act in conjunction with his prescribed nightly dose and it wasn't enough to kill him outright. And she hadn't counted on the effect of adrenaline.

Charles felt something warm and wet touching him, like a cat licking his hand. He struggled to wake. He had to get to Helene, had to tell her something, something vital. But the drugs sapped at his strength and fought him. It wasn't until something with a wooden handle was pressed into his hand that he was able to open his eyes.

Jacob was crouched over him. He was wearing his great coat and there were dark stains on his sheet-white face. He was forcing something into Charles' hand and froze when he saw that Charles' eyes were open. It was then that Charles realized that the stains on his face were blood spatters. And Charles, in his innocence, thought, *He's been hurt.*

"Jacob…" he croaked.

Jacob fled, running to the wardrobe, pulling at his great coat, panicking and frightened. Charles struggled to sit up, but he was too slow and Jacob was gone before he gained his feet.

He saw what had been placed into his now-bloodied hand. The razor was still wet. His shirt was stained too, smudged with blood where Jacob's hands had been. He couldn't understand, didn't understand. Didn't, that is, until he saw what was left of his wife…

Charles reeled and Johnny did too. The collective pain brought them back into the present with a rush.

I was too slow to understand... Charles was weeping. *Too slow, and it cost me everything. You can't wait, Johnny. You can't.*

Sweat streamed down Johnny's face as he tried to catch his breath. The crush of grief and guilt was nearly overwhelming and he still had the door to face.

The door to the passage was open and the darkness beckoned, like an intoxicating drink laced with poison. This was a conscious darkness, alive and starving. Johnny knew that it would devour him whole if it could.

It reached for him and he recoiled.

It's the only way, Charles said. He was begging now, pleading with Johnny. *Release me, oh, release me, save us, save us...*

But Johnny could not, would not, he simply could not face it again, not the dark, not alone, not again, not now, not so soon-

That was when he heard Linda.

It was just a gasp, just a whispered, "*No,*" but he heard it and he recognized it.

Linda.

It has her, Charles said. *I cannot help you here. It is the province of the living.*

Just like that, Charles was gone. Johnny never knew whether he had simply left or if Johnny himself had thrown him out, but it did not matter. The darkness beckoned. Johnny plunged into it.

CHAPTER 33

The staircase curved around in a circular fashion, old, rickety and shrouded in gloom as thick as swamp water. It resisted penetration and fought Johnny for every step. He did not pause or wait. He pressed forward and even the darkness could not hold out against his will.

By the second bend of the staircase he saw the light, pale, unnatural, and more ominous than the shadows. With the light came sound: Linda, whimpering, hurt.

He staggered up the next couple of stairs and stopped.

Linda was there, hanging suspended in midair, her hands at her throat as though struggling against a choking grip. Her eyes were wide and blank with terror. She was staring straight ahead, but there was nothing to see.

Johnny found his voice.

"Linda!"

She did not answer, did not move. Something hissed loudly. The air lashed out at him, striking him across the face. It was only a weak blow. The concentration was on Linda who cried out and went up another inch or two. Her body twisted in pain.

"Let her go," Johnny demanded.

A snicker echoed through the room. Linda gurgled. From overhead, they heard a slow, steady pounding, like a battering ram against a sturdy castle door. Linda's body twisted in tension, then relaxed. The movement of her legs drew Johnny's eyes downward. On the stairs under her feet lay a battered, stained coat.

Suddenly, Charles was there again, his memories assailing Johnny: the party, the long drive from Boston, the ringing of the front doorbell through all the noise and chatter. Jacob coming in, grave as always, knocking the snow from his coat – that coat. There came another flash of the memory cards: Charles, in the ballroom, staring past the shocked party guests to out the wide bay windows. Jacob was hurrying away from the house. He wasn't wearing the coat. Another flash and Charles was outside, on the dock, struggling to keep his feet. Jacob was turning, his eyes wide with panic. He lifted his hands to deflect the blow. There were red stains on the cuffs of his sleeves.

Charles receded and Johnny looked up.

"That's you, Irene, isn't it?" he asked.

The air hissed again and Linda made a croaking sound.

Johnny pressed, "You're trying to protect your husband, Jacob, aren't you? The man you agreed to marry when you realized that you couldn't actually get the lord of the manor, right?"

The hissing sound grew.

He gained courage and took a step further. "Wasn't it your idea to kill Charles, Irene? You told Jacob it was for the business, but wasn't it also to get back at the man who'd turned you down? You made Jacob kill Helene, but Charles was your responsibility."

The light was changing. Shadows mixed in it like storm clouds preparing for a hurricane. The air grew icier. Irene's was a will of iron. She would not give.

Johnny pressed, "If *you* had killed Helene, you would have been cleverer with the coat. You would have made sure it hadn't been left behind. The truth of the matter is that Jacob just isn't as strong or as cool as you. He left it here and that's why you kept hounding Rachel to come back. You needed to get the coat. What happened ten years ago, Irene? Did Helene come back to frighten you? Was it Charles that chased you down the stairs and made you fall?"

The storm was growing, building. Linda looked as frail as a china doll, shaking in the grip of a dangerous force. The pounding continued, echoing in the narrow chamber like a death knell – pound – pound – pound.

Johnny raised his voice: he was almost shouting now. "It was all for nothing, Irene. We *know* and the truth will get out. Even if you kill Linda and me, you can't hide the coat or this passage any longer. There are other people here and they will know. We're going to take the coat and expose you and there's nothing you can do about it, Irene. You've lost."

Her shriek ripped through the atmosphere, slamming into him like a fist to the face. He fell back against the wall. When he looked up again, dazed, the light had changed, whirling about like mad while Linda, awake from her terrified stupor, shrieked and fought against the invisible grip.

The memories came back in full force. It was as though all the darkness in the house, all the blackness in his own soul, all the torment that he had faced and buried in the past five years came back to life to attack him. Into the black hole he fell, the faces of those he'd killed and seen killed mixing with memories of blood and ash. Doubts, denials, defeat, hatred, and putrid condemnation, always festering below the surface, rose up in force against him. He fought the ebony tide. It was like drowning, but it was worse. It was drowning without the relief of death.

He was drowning, but he fought back…and this time, Johnny won.

Just as he was declaring victory, the black tide disappeared and he was back on the staircase again. Only now there were three of them; himself, Linda, still suspended, and Irene.

The light had turned and congealed into the figure of a thin woman with a long face contorted by defeat and hatred. She stood unnaturally tall in the vestiges of an old robe, her hair loose and untidy and her hands clenched into fists. Though she was not touching Linda, there was no doubt that it was she who was holding her.

It was not until she turned to Johnny that he saw her eyes. Or rather, he saw where her eyes ought to have been. They were not there anymore, only terrible empty wells where eyes should have been.

Johnny thought, *Of course - eyes are the window to the soul.*

She was bearing down on him, her hair flying around her and her expression horrifyingly determined. The hissing sound had returned, accompanied by a rushing sound, like all the moans of all the defeated of the world. The sound grew. He could barely hear the pounding of the man trying to break through the paneling upstairs.

For a moment, he wavered.

Her will is too strong.

Then Linda uttered a small, terrified cry, audible even over the roaring sound of Irene's displeasure.

Johnny drew himself up and faced her.

"You have no place here, Irene Simmons North," he shouted. "Your secret is out. There is nothing to hide anymore. You are defeated. We win."

She was almost on top of him now, her anger lashing out in powerful waves of wind and sound, but he would not bend.

"I *command* you to leave, Irene."

He remembered his troops, the respect they gave him, even when the situation went south. He thought of Linda and all the hours she had spent nursing him through his nightmares. He thought of Charles and Helene and his stomach clenched tight at the memory.

"You've caused enough trouble around here," he shouted. "You cannot have me or anyone else today. In the name of all that is holy, I command you to go!"

She roared and she screamed. The house shuddered. Wood groaned and strained. Linda's back was arcing. The pounding noise grew more fervent but Johnny could barely hear it above the roar. Wills clashed and the turmoil was great. He felt as though the universe were being rent in two and that he and Linda were about to be shattered into pieces so small and scattered that no one would ever find them again. When he heard the shattering noise of wood and a hinge giving away, he thought it was the staircase and all he could think was, *Susan and Michael are safe at least.*

Then, like an extinguished candle, it was all over.

Irene disappeared and the wind, the light, and Johnny's remaining strength went with her. Linda shouted as she plummeted. Bill Emery, who had just plowed through the upstairs doorway, was there to catch her before she hit the stairs.

"What the hell was that?" he called out.

Johnny, sagging against the wall, his eyes streaming, had no strength left to answer him.

CHAPTER 34

In the living room, Susan's wild French mumblings subsided abruptly. She was sitting up, grasping Michael's hand as though to prevent him from leaving. Her wide, empty eyes never left his face until the moment her chatter stopped.

She cocked her head as though to listen. Michael, watching her, got the eerie sensation that he was not watching his wife, but rather a mannequin made up to look like her.

What she was listening to Michael did not know. He glanced around the room as though by looking he might be better able to hear what she heard. Then he realized that Johnny had disappeared.

His heart jumped in his throat and he thought, *How long has he been gone? Long enough to…?*

Susan's long shuddering sigh caught his attention. She fell back against the couch and the pinched expression on her face relaxed. She looked relieved but she still did not look like Susan and when she spoke, it was in French.

He became really alarmed then and snapped, "Susan, *stop* it!"

To his surprise, she did. She swallowed hard, twice and squeezed his hands in a comforting manner.

"It is… all right," she said, but the heavily accented voice was not Susan's. "It is all right now. She is gone. You are safe. She is safe now. The baby — she wanted…"

She bit her lip and looked away from him in sudden pain. Then she looked at him again, this time with kindness.

"It will be well." she said. "I saved her for you. You and your family will tell the truth and it will be well. You were good to come. Tell Rachel, she was right, yes? She was right."

The door to the den blew open. Michael, his nerves as taut as a bow string, jumped up to his feet. There was no one, nothing, at the door but a chill draft and the scent of cinnamon and cloves. Then the breeze and the scent were gone and they were alone.

Susan sighed. She had fallen back against the pillows of the coach. And when she opened her eyes, she was Susan again.

EPILOGUE

The storm blew away as quickly as it had come. Christmas Eve dawned clear, crisp, and beautiful, the kind of day that Bing Crosby would have ordered, Michael said. Emery, who had not slept for most of the night, advised him that it was too early on a coffee-less morning for such cheery declarations.

They discovered that Emery's radio was working again. Emery messaged the local sheriff who immediately dispatched the plowman and called Susan's parents to let them know that their daughter and her companions were all right. As soon as the local doctor had taken a good look at everyone, Emery would deliver the foursome to their doorstep.

Michael protested, "It's an awfully long drive, Emery!"

Emery shrugged. "Yeah, well, it'll get me out of wrapping presents and making small talk with the aunts for a few hours. That alone will be worth it."

Linda did not believe this explanation and told him that she thought he was a good angel. Emery told her to stop talking nonsense.

It was seven in the morning before the street was plowed enough to drive. Johnny and Emery, with some little help from Michael, dug Emery's car out of the snow and somehow managed to shove all the essential luggage and gifts into his trunk. Emery himself took charge of Jacob's coat.

"This is evidence," he said. "Local sheriff has jurisdiction. But don't worry – the DA's a good guy. There's a case here and he'll follow it up."

Michael hoped so.

"In a way," he said to Susan, as he was settling her into the car, "it was a good thing we came here. If we hadn't, we might never have known about the passageway or found that coat. The bulldozers would have come and destroyed everything. As it is, when the board learns what we've discovered, regardless of what the DA decides to do, the Reynolds' Company is going to be looking for a new president."

"Yes," Susan said, absently. She was looking across the street. Michael's car was just a pile of snow from which a homemade flag flew limply. "Do you think we came here? Or were we *called* here?"

Michael shivered at the thought and rubbed his sore arm. The aching had dulled in the past few hours, but the pain was bone-deep. Even if it wasn't broken, he'd probably lost the use of it for a week or two.

Looking at Susan and thinking about the events of the past night, he considered it a small price to pay for their safety.

"If we were called here," he said, after a moment, "at least we were called by family...family that looked after us, even if they did total my car."

She looked up at him and smiled.

Linda opened the door on the other side of the car and slid into the front passenger seat. She was breathless and holding something in her hand.

"I stole something," she said and showed them the music box. "I figured Rachel wouldn't mind."

Linda looked radiant.

Susan shivered and thought, *She is* never *playing that thing in my house.*

***

Emery was the last to leave the house. He took one more look around to make sure that the place was empty, and it was. The halls echoed only with the sound of his own footsteps, and when there was a draft, there was a corresponding gap in the wall to account for it. Still, it was with a sense of relief that he left the building and snapped a padlock on the front door.

He had already spoken to the sheriff about the Reynolds' case. The sheriff was going to call the DA and meet Emery and the others at the doctor's office to take the coat and get their statements for the record.

"DA will like this, Bill," he had said. "He's looking to run for governor sometime. Shutting down Reynolds' Corporation will make him look like a mighty big man."

"Yeah," Emery said, "just don't expect coherent statements today, Frank. The kids here have had a rough night."

"Why, did they run into that ghost the locals are always going on about?"

The sheriff laughed and Emery did, too. When he signed off, he thought, *No one is going to believe this at the precinct.*

However, it *had* happened and Emery knew it. He did not like ghosts or the supernatural, but he had seen Irene, felt her presence, and saw, if only briefly, the battle of wills on the staircase. He was not the type to deny what he had seen with his own eyes.

Still, if he never encountered a thing like this again, Bill Emery would be a very happy man.

Johnny was waiting for him on the porch, hands shoved deep into his pockets against the cold of the winter's day. His face was drawn and white and when he looked at Emery, it was with haunted eyes.

Emery nodded at him. "Tight as a drum. Let's go get you some breakfast. You look like you need it."

Johnny nodded and his eyes darted past Emery to the somber house settling behind them.

Johnny Vincent had his own concerns and fears. For a few brief, wonderful hours, he had been free from the darkness and the nightmares that had constantly plagued him. It was as though his confrontation with Irene had been, in truth, a man-to-man faceoff with his darker side. He had won last night, but that had been because Linda was in danger and it was only with considerable cost to himself. Now he found himself wondering: when the darkness returned, when the nightmares resumed, which of course they must, how could he face them again? How could he go back?

He was startled by Emery's hand, clapping down hard on his shoulder.

"You did good in there, kid," Emery. "What you did took guts."

Johnny laughed, a short, haunted sound. "It's easy to face what you can see. It's what you can't see that really terrifies me."

Emery looked at the house, then at Johnny.

"War touches a man, son," he said simply, without condescension, one soldier to another. "We all bring a bit of the darkness home with us. But it only ever has the power that we allow it. In the end we have the final say on how much control it has. You told that witch in there to take a powder. Anyone who can do that can tell the nightmares to do the same and the nightmares will listen."

Johnny stared at him and knew then that he was right. It was as though chains had fallen off his soul and he could stand upright again. He was stronger than his memories and he could, with time, create new ones, good ones, to compete with the old.

Gratitude welled up inside him. Before he could respond, Emery had started off for the car, yelling over his shoulder, "Will you hurry up, soldier boy? This old man has to eat before he becomes a ghost!"

John Vincent grinned and ran after him.

ABOUT THE AUTHORS

Margaret Traynor and **Killarney Traynor** are sisters who live in New Hampshire and have way too much time on their hands. **Margaret** is an EA, travel enthusiast, and coffee fanatic who works in an accounting office during the day and hikes the White Mountains on the weekends. **Killarney** is an author, actress, and bookworm and generally too busy watching black and white movies to hike. *Tale Half Told* is the first book The Encounter Series.

For more information about The Encounter Series, or to contact the Traynor sisters, please visit www.killarneytraynor.com.